CHASING BLACK ICE

Don't miss any of Doc Ephraim Bates'
exciting comedic action thrillers

Boom!!...Killers. Series
Chasing Black Ice
Chasing Revenge
Chasing Liberation
Chasing Redemption

Dragon's Men Series
Dragon's Men: Domestic

CHASING BLACK ICE

Boom!!...Killers.

SERIES BOOK #1

Doc Ephraim Bates

Golden Alley Press
Emmaus, Pennsylvania

Golden Alley Press
37 South 6th Street
Emmaus, Pennsylvania 18049

www.goldenalleypress.com

Golden Alley Press books may be purchased for educational, business, or sales promotional use. For information please contact the publisher.

Printed in the United States of America

Chasing Black Ice: Boom!!...Killers. series book #1 / Doc Ephraim Bates.

ISBN 978-0-9895265-8-6 print
ISBN 978-0-9895265-9-3 ebook

Back cover photograph of the author ©Michael J. Hoffman

Cover design by Michael Sayre

10 9 8 7 6 5 4 3

This book is dedicated to Laurie Shen.
Thank you for always calling me back.
Eph.

THE SMELL OF RAIN

<pre>
          SUMMERTIME
       FRIDAY EVENING
DOWNTOWN WASHINGTON, D.C.
</pre>

It was a little after 6:30 p.m. as Harper Rowe walked down the sidewalk of G Street NW. With a tuxedo in a protective clothing bag slung over his left shoulder, he was headed to the apartment of his best friend, Kinley Devereaux.

Harper hated coming down here on weekends. That was when the ne'er-do-wells took all his favorite secret parking spots. This evening he had to park some 17 blocks away from Kinley's place.

Normally Harper did not mind the walk, but tonight with every block he trekked, the tuxedo he was hauling on his back seemed to become heavier and heavier. To boot, the D.C. skies were growing increasingly gray as a summer thunderstorm threatened to unload on the District. But he was pretty sure he had enough time to make it to Kinley's apartment before the skies opened up. As he closed in on the final two blocks, he looked ahead and up toward his buddy's 18th floor apartment and saw him standing out on the balcony.

Harper shifted the tuxedo across to his right shoulder, grabbed his cell phone out of his left pants pocket, and dialed his good friend.

"Harper?" Devereaux answered on the first ring. "Where the heck are you? We got about thirty minutes till we have to hit it – and please don't give me the ole 'It's cool to be fashionably late' routine because this isn't some backwoods bar-b-que we're going to, Bro. This is the freakin' Under Secretary of Defense we're talking about here. Two things you don't want to be late for in this lifetime are a breakfast buffet with Jethro Bodine and this."

"Relax, Kin, I got you in my sights as we speak. And I take offense at the 'backwoods' comment. I live in White Marsh, man. Hardly what I'd call the back woods."

"Right. Sorry. I forgot you moved since we last spoke. I'm still used to you living in Delta, Pennsylvania, which – if I'm not mistaken – is still considered backwoods."

By now Harper was standing in front of Kinley's building, staring straight up the 18 floors at his best friend on his balcony.

"Hey, Kin, you got a quarter? You should drop it down and let it hit my head. See if it causes any damage. You know, the old science experiment – I wanna see if it really hurts."

"Actually, I'm fresh out of quarters, but I do have a bowling ball in my closet. I can drop that down on your head and see what happens."

"Ha Ha, you're a riot, Ramona. Buzz me in, if ya don't mind. This tux is a rental and I can smell rain in the air."

Boom!!...Killer.

By the time Harper had ridden the elevator to the 18th floor, made his way down the hall to Kinley's apartment, and let himself in, the skies really had opened up. It was pouring.

Inside, the two friends were embracing and patting each other on the back. Kinley pulled away. "Easy, bud, I'm a little sore from my last trip."

"You get hit?"

"Nah," Kinley smiled. "Sunburn. Waikiki can get really sunny in the afternoons."

"Waikiki? Hawaii?"

"No, jackass, Waikiki, Wisconsin."

"Ah, man," Rowe whined, "you always get the good assignments. I don't know why Kelly hates me so much. Or is it that she loves you?"

"Ah, c'mon, Harp. You were in Hong Kong. How cool was that? I mean, really, how did that go?"

"Really?" Harper asked incredulously. "You're going to compare Hong Kong to Waikiki? Ya know what, Kin, you're like a VISA card: You're everywhere *I* want to be."

"Take it easy, green-eyed monster. Seriously, how was your trip?"

Harper tossed his tuxedo down on Kinley's couch and shook his head. "You won't—"

"Believe what happened this time," Devereaux finished his friend's sentence. "Let me guess. You were nearly caught – got out through some back door – met some lonely, homeless girl that you had relations with – blah, blah, blah. Am I close?"

"No. Not even." Off Harper went into his latest tale of tumult and turmoil. "My mark was staying in this high class, Grade A hotel. There was no scaling this mother or trying to cut through the window glass. Nothing like that." He inhaled for a moment. "So, I did the usual: staked out the hotel lobby and waited to find out what room the guy was in – Room 213, for the record. Then I wait for him to go out and I go up to his room. I pull out my magic hotel key and..."

The "magic hotel key" that Harper was speaking of was an electronic key card custom made for him by an ex-Brazilian black ops guy that he knew from a previous trip to Carnivale in Rio de Janeiro. The key card opened 98% of all hotel room doors across the world. Harper did not know how it worked, nor did he care. All he knew was that he paid the guy 50 large for it, and it was the best investment he had ever made.

"...Voila, I'm in. I got the place to myself for who knows how long so I start searching—"

"Lemme guess. For some shoes?"

"Why must you always interrupt me at the good parts?"

Kinley moved over to the stove where he had some water boiling for tea. "Because some of your stories have the same elements in them." He took the kettle off the stove and placed it on the counter. "But, by all means, go on." Without looking up from pouring the boiling water into a white teacup, he said dryly, "I hope I didn't interrupt. As you were."

"No shoes."

Devereaux set the kettle down long enough to look at his friend. "What do you mean, 'no shoes'?"

"No shoes," Rowe repeated. "No shoes, no slippers, no flip-flops, sandals, gators, sneakers, no moccasins, no loafers, no freakin' footwear of any kind in any part of the hotel room. Nothing, Kin."

"So what did you do?"

"Well, what could I do? I mean, I use a technique that's proven and practically foolproof. Plus, I'm in the room and in the middle of the production – it's not like I could just call a mulligan and come back later – so I did the one thing that I could do."

"And what was that?"

"Well, I had to wait. I had to wait for when I knew there *was* going to be some sort of footwear in the place. Obviously, the guy's wearing something on his feet. It's cold in Hong Kong this time of year. So, I camped out under the bed, and I waited."

By now Kinley had carried his tea over to the island that separated his living room from the kitchen area and seated himself atop of one of the two wooden bar stools that tucked under the island. After taking a careful sip of his hot beverage, he said sarcastically, "Well, it's good to know that you didn't find it beneath yourself to resort to such second grade tactics as hiding under a bed. You know, true professional that you are."

"We do what we must," Harper shrugged. "So, as if things aren't going screwy enough as it is, I'm under the bed for about three freaking hours. I'm taking little catnaps – waking up every time I hear footsteps outside the room in the hall. I'm going over in my head alternate ways out of the room if things get really squirrelly. Eventually, I start thinking this prick may not even be coming back to the room at all. It's getting to be well after 2 a.m., but I wait a little longer, and, finally, the jackass comes back, drunk as a skunk, with two Asian ladies of the night. One tucked under each arm. They're pretty tanked, too."

"Things are getting interesting now." Devereaux smiled a wry smile.

"Oh yeah, buddy, it gets interesting all right. Clothes start coming off – shirts, blouses, bras – as the three of them start positioning themselves on the bed. Still, the guy's got his shoes on, and things are really starting to happen up there. The bed's sagging in the middle and making things very uncomfortable for me. I'm doing my darndest not to grunt or moan, ya know, because I'm getting pancaked down there. Then, at last, the shoes come off…as well as the pants and other various garments. But it's perfect; the shoes are sitting right by the side of the bed, well within my reach. Or so I thought."

"Meaning?"

"Did I mention the part about my mark being all of about three hundred pounds of pure whale blubber? And it's right about this time that he and his lady friends are floundering around on top of the bed like a bunch of polar bears on a trampoline. Every time I go to reach for the shoes, Fatty McChubville and the Chang sisters have their sexual pendulum on the down swing, and it's spot welding me into the carpet."

"Spot welding? Well, maybe next time you set up shop under a hotel bed you'll be sure to wear a flak jacket, huh?" Kin took a quick peek at his wristwatch. "We wrapping this yarn up any time soon, chief? We are on a bit of a schedule here."

"Right, right. So, eventually, after I finally get my hands on the shoes, I pull out TINA and dump her inside Bluto's shoes…"

TINA was the pet name for Harper Rowe's tool of choice. It is a deadly poison that is equal parts thalamic acid and sodium. The thalamic acid is the deadly part, and the sodium is what masks it in the bloodstream to make it undetectable to even the best of medical examiners. In chemical equation shorthand, it is $T1Na$ – or, as Harper Rowe was fond of calling it: TINA.

What Harper liked to do was to find a target's shoe, dump a small amount of TINA into the empty shoe, and wait for the target to slide his or her foot into it.

The fastest way into a person's bloodstream is through the bottom of the foot. It's why heroin addicts shoot up in between their toes. The heroin enters the bloodstream through the foot, and – zing! – it's on the fast track to the heart and brain. If someone is using heroin, it's great – hello, great high – but if it's thalamic acid and sodium that is hitting the bloodstream at warp speed, then things do not end up nearly as well. In fact, things just end. Period.

Once Harper Rowe's targets put on their TINA-tainted footwear, it usually took between 30 to 40 minutes before they dropped dead from an apparent heart attack. To Harper, TINA was the perfect weapon: quiet, effective, reliable. And left the scene without a trace.

"And then I just crawled up toward the headboard, listened to the festivities, and waited for the morning."

Kinley stood up and started walking toward his room. "Well, I'm glad you got the blind man's view of a threesome, and I am truly happy that you got your mark and made it out alive, but time's—"

"Hold on, boss," Harper said as he stepped in front of his buddy. "We're not done yet. Just give me two more minutes," Harper held up two fingers. "Just two. You're gonna love this."

"Geez, it just never ends with you, does it?"

"I know. I know. We're on a timeframe – but here's what happens next. You're gonna love this."

Devereaux walked back to his seat, sat down, and resumed listening to his friend's story.

"So, I spend the next few hours catching some shut eye, under the headboard, out of harm's way. The two call girls leave around 6 a.m., and the tub o' lard that is my mark, he gets out of the sack around two hours later. He puts on his shoes – apparently they're some kind of all-purpose footwear, even better for me – he walks into the bathroom, does something, and then I hear a thud."

Kinley, who had backed away from his buddy and returned to his seat, gave Harper a curious look. "So, what? The guy was walking around in TINA for – like 30 seconds, and then he dropped?"

"I crawl out from underneath the bed and go in to look at the dude. He's just laying on the bathroom floor not moving, and from what I can tell…not breathing."

"No way TINA worked that fast."

"Well, no kidding, Agatha Christie," Rowe smarted off. "So, I go in and check for a pulse, some sort of breathing, anything."

"And–?"

"And nothing. The guy's dead from a massive heart attack. Well, I know TINA's not even close to being in his system, and it's not like I can just leave it as it is. My orders – as always – are to not leave a trace that I, or anybody else, have been there. That's my specialty. No blood, no violence, no trace of any forensic evidence. Yet, here I am staring at this dead guy that, apparently, wore out his heart with those two Asian chicks. And I'm thinking to myself, I have *to stinking un-assassinate this guy!*"

Kinley, with an evil grin on his face, says, "You're right, Harp. I *am* loving this." Devereaux took another sip from his teacup. "So, what did you do? What *could* you do?"

"Well, I'll tell you what I did. I took his mother loving shoes, for one thing. Then I grabbed a rag and some soap, and I washed the bottom of his feet. Then, in desperation, I grabbed the coffee packets that were in the room, and rubbed them up and down his feet."

"What did you do that for?"

"Coffee grounds, babe!" Harper looked at Kinley like he was totally missing the point. "Colombians use it to hide the smell of cocaine. I just figured it would hide any type of smell that TINA left behind."

"Does TINA leave a smell?"

"I don't know," said an exasperated Harper Rowe. "Usually it just kills and then disappears. But I wasn't taking any chances."

"And then?" asked Devereaux.

"And then, his all-purpose shoes in hand, I calmly walked out of there. Out of the room, into the elevator, off the elevator onto the ground floor, through the lobby, out the door, and into a cab. Caught the first flight home…and here I am."

Kinley stood up, his teacup empty. "Are you done?"

"Not yet. Just before I came over, I was watching CNN. They were talking about my mark – found dead in a hotel bathroom yesterday. After an autopsy, the official cause of death: massive heart attack. I officially un-assassinated my guy."

Kinley took his teacup into the kitchen area and placed it in the sink. "Well, I'm proud of you for your un-assassination. Another piece of fine work on your behalf. Now…would you care to hear about my assignment?"

"Sure. Lay it on me."

"Well, it went a little bit like this: I found a good position on a rooftop, put my rifle to my shoulder, lined up my mark through my scope, and – boom!!…killer." Kinley walked past his good friend and patted him on the back. "See, Harp, they just pay me to *kill* – not for style points – and I'm really good at it."

"Let's get dressed. We're late," Harper Rowe said flatly as he looked out the window of Devereaux's apartment.

The rain had stopped.

Bad

Tara Madison had made a lot of money in her short lifetime. She, literally, had millions of dollars stashed away in bank accounts all over the world, most of them in Switzerland, where her money could neither be stolen, frozen, nor taxed.

Despite her tremendous amount of wealth, Tara chose to live the life of a minimalist. She drove a beat-up '96 Dodge pickup truck, dressed like your everyday tomboy, and lived in a barely-furnished row house on the north side of Washington D.C.

In her line of work, it was hard enough to attain anonymity – man's world that it was – by being one of the lone females in the mercenary business. She did not need to attract any extra attention her way by living a garish, luxurious lifestyle that was way outside of her supposed means.

This evening, she sat at the foot of her single bed, reading the note that had been left in her mailbox in an unmarked envelope. It simply read:

> **1127 Garrison Park Drive**
> **Contents in Upstairs Lockbox**
> **Meet team in cross street basement**
> **Money will be wired to account upon delivery**

Tara balled up the piece of paper and stood up. Pulling a lighter from the front pants pocket of her faded blue jeans, she made her way into the kitchen. She stumbled a little bit as she ignited the note and dropped it into the kitchen sink. She watched impatiently as the piece of paper burned itself out. Turning on the spigot, she washed the ashes down the drain.

The other specifics of this particular job, such as time and date, what was to be taken, and the coordinating drop point, had been set and sent well over two months earlier. The details had been released to its participants over a six-month period. Some by packages left on porches, some by anonymous texts from throw-away cell phones, some by mysterious blank envelopes that showed up in mailboxes – much like the message Tara had received today – but none of the details had been delivered in any way that could ever be traced back to their original sender.

Garrison Park was one of the most upscale suburbs of the District and was called home by some of the wealthiest and most powerful men – and women – in the world. The security on its streets was always tight just because of the clientele that lived in the neighborhood.

Sometimes it did not matter how dangerous the street a person lived on was. Sometimes it just mattered if that street was the address of someone who could contribute to the mayor's slush fund. And the streets in Garrison Park were lined with some major contributors.

To most thieves, this would have been a deterrent. But tonight, Tara Madison knew it was in her favor.

❄   ❄   ❄

Dressed to the nines in their tuxedos, Harper Rowe and Kinley Devereaux took the elevator from Devereaux's apartment down to the parking garage that housed Kinley's soft-top Corvette. The two men stepped off the elevator and strode confidently toward the car.

"I gotta say, Kin, you look like a million bucks."

Devereaux looked at his friend. "You, too, Harp. We're golden."

"Like a graham. Are we going to put the top down this evening?"

"Screw that. It's been raining. I'm not gonna drive down the street and let water get splashed all over my leather interior. Besides, we look good. No need messing up our hair and clothes."

"Okay," Harper hesitated a bit. "I guess you make a good point."

"Just get in already," Devereaux said as he opened the driver's side door and got in. "We're about twenty minutes later than I wanted to be. We gotta make up some time."

Harper opened his door and got into the passenger side seat. He looked at his buddy and asked, "Do you know where we're going?"

"I do not…but I do have the address, and all I have to do is put it into my phone here, and we'll be fine." Devereaux carefully entered the address: 1127 Garrison Park Drive.

Very Bad Things

In the grand scheme of things, the only thing tighter than peas in a pod is… jail buddies. There is nothing like them.

Army buddies always had their time at war. High school buddies always had their time at youth. Movie buddies always had their time at the show.

But jail buddies – they always had their time at figuring things out.

Jason Kilpatrick and Dustin Vargas had been prison buddies for about three or four months. Not long, but long enough to figure out a few things. Jason knew a few people, and Dustin knew a few other people.

They both knew that, once they were out of jail, they would keep in touch just in case a job came up. Jason's buddies would somehow contact Dustin's buddies…and so on and so forth.

A few weeks ago, Jason Kilpatrick and Dustin Vargas had been released from prison. A few days ago, Jason's buddies contacted Dustin's buddies. Tonight, Jason and Dustin reunited in a basement across the street from 1127 Garrison Park Drive. And they were champing at the bit to find out what to do next. They stood confidently next to each other as they looked around at the other seven members in the room.

Tara Madison drove her Dodge pickup slowly through the upscale neighborhood of Little River Village until she came upon 1127 Garrison Park Drive. She slowed down just slightly as she got to what would be her point of attack. Through her passenger side window she saw the huge mansion that was surrounded by tall security walls with black wrought-iron fences at every entrance. Turning her head quickly, she looked out her driver's side window to the cross-street abode where she would be meeting her allies for tonight's job. The huge home was currently undergoing major renovations. It was easy to see that the renovations were such a large undertaking that the residents would certainly be staying elsewhere, and at this time of night, the renovators would be long gone, too. Tara drove up the street a ways to park her truck out of sight from any curious onlookers, and began her trek back to the rendezvous point.

They heard a basement door slam shut.

Kilpatrick and Vargas waited with bated breath for the one that was going to give them their marching orders for this evening.

Tara Madison strode into the basement, looked around the room, and said, "I'm here to do a job. Anyone that's not here to do a job… you're welcome to leave." She looked around the room.

Everyone in the basement looked around at everyone else, and stood still.

"In that case," Madison said sternly and without prejudice, "I'll assume that we are all in. Ladies and gentlemen, this a good chance to make some easy money. I've got the plan of execution for this operation. As long as everybody does what they're supposed to do, we'll all be very rich in a matter of just a week. Now," she reached into her pants pocket and pulled out a slip of paper, "which one of you is…" she unfolded the paper and read the name she had scribbled down, "… Jason Kilpatrick?"

"I am," said a tall, redheaded, red-bearded man that was standing off to Madison's left.

"You're the safecracker?"

"I am."

"Then you will be accompanying me into the house," Tara said. She spent the next 20 minutes going over the plan with everyone else – every point of attack with each man and woman until she was satisfied that everyone knew what each of them had to do to make tonight's operation a success. When she was finished, the team waited patiently until it was time for them to do some very bad things.

The Faithful Man

For most people, the way Kinley Devereaux was swerving in and out of downtown D.C. traffic would have been cause for a major artery explosion. However, Harper Rowe had ridden with some of the worst drivers in the world, and the way Kinley was driving this evening was, at most, slightly reckless. Harper had not even bothered to put on his seatbelt. The two men rode in silence for the first 10 minutes of the drive while Porcupine Tree played on the CD player. Finally, after Kinley found himself stuck at a seemingly everlasting red light, he turned down the music to ask his friend a question.

"So, you're a religious man, right?"

"No, I am not. I'm a faithful man."

Harper's response was met by the electronic female voice coming from Kinley's navigation system – *stay in the left hand lane and turn left in one-half mile.* As he swerved around a slow-moving SUV, Kinley said, "I was not aware that there was a difference. Enlighten me, oh, enlightened one."

"Well, there's a lot of religious people out there, Kin, but sadly, so few that have actual faith. It's that age-old quandary, ya know. Everybody wants to go to heaven, but no one wants to die."

"Meaning–?"

"Religious people are the ones that talk a good game, go to church every weekend and sometimes during the week, cling to their morals and principles when it's convenient, and think it's all good."

"Okay, so what's the spin? Why are you different?"

–Turn left in one-quarter mile.

"Let me tell you a story, buddy. It goes like this: a religious man and a faithful man are standing close to the edge of a cliff. Suddenly, the ground gives way and they both fall over the edge. About halfway down, the two men pass a branch that is jutting out from the cliff wall, and they both grab onto it. Safe for the moment, they start yelling incessantly as they cling tight to the branch. Finally, after a few minutes they hear a voice from the top of the cliff saying, 'It's okay. I'm here to help you. It's me, God.' Both men are grateful, and the faithful man asks 'What do we need to do?' And God replies, 'Let go and everything will be okay.' So the faithful man lets go, and the religious man asks, 'Is there anyone else up there that can help us?' And, that my good friend, is the difference between a faithful man and a religious man."

Kinley chuckled a bit, "Okay, so I see what you're saying. But, here's my question to you, faithful man: Do you think that what we do is wrong? All the killing? All the bloodshed that we dispel on the world? Does it ever weigh on your conscience?"

–Turn left ahead.

Harper laughed at his friend. "Really? After all the time that we've known each other – you're asking that question now?"

"I've wanted to ask it before, but I guess I just never got around to it."

–Turn left here.

"No, Kinny, it doesn't ever weigh on my conscience. The way I see it, guys like you and me that are blessed with the talents that we've been given, we could kill anyone, anywhere, anytime – and walk away scot-free. Now that would be wrong. But we don't do that, do we? We use our talents to take out the world's trash. Tyrants, despots, pimps, dictator – all the people that cause harm to the world's greater good."

–Turn right in one-tenth of a mile.

"Yeah, I like that, Harp. That's good. I suppose you're right. Maybe I'll be able to sleep a little better tonight. I haven't let it get to me before, but recently, it's started playin' around in my head a bit." Kinley took a right onto the next road before he asked, "So, whatever happened to the two men – the faithful man and the religious man?"

"The faithful man fell and landed in rushing waters that washed him up onto the banks of a mighty river. He got up and walked away. The religious man – he's still holding on to that branch waiting for someone else to come up to the top of the cliff and save him."

–You have reached your destination.

THE PARTY

Under Secretary of Defense Doug Hopkins was ready to throw the biggest party of the summer. It was the talk of the D.C. town. Rumors had even swirled that the Vice President of the United States himself was going to be in attendance.

The party was a big deal, to be sure, with all the delegates, senators, congressmen, and ambassadors that might be in attendance. Knowing the security that someone like the Vice President was going to bring, Hopkins had backed down his own security. Despite the protests of his secretary and most of his colleagues, he was not too terribly concerned with any outside threats. He did not want his guests to feel like they were in any sort of danger. Besides, those who felt like they were in any sort of peril were allowed to bring their own security detail.

With all the guests that had brought their own security, and all the questions and double-checking that went along with it, the doorman at Doug Hopkins' abode was happy to see Kinley Devereaux show up with just a single invitation, no guests, no security.

"Hey, buddy," Kin said to the guard at the door, "better pat down the guy behind me. I heard him talking in the parking lot. I think he's some kind of nut job." While the doorman's apprentices were in the middle of patting down Kinley Devereaux, they stopped immediately to move to Harper Rowe.

"Easy kids," Harper said as he held up his own invitation. "I got admission to the ball, too. Though you might want to check my friend for a glass slipper and a pumpkin shoved up his tailpipe."

After receiving a thorough pat down, both two men entered the house of Doug Hopkins and the biggest party of the summer. They looked around in awe at the size of the place. "Look at this, Harp. This is the biggest house I've ever seen."

"I know. And this is just the mud room."

On either side of the huge foyer there was a case of semi-spiraled stairs that led up to the second floor. Two security guards stood in front of the steps, one on each side.

"Wonder what they got up there?"

"Don't even try to find out, Harper."

"Hey, Kin," Rowe whispered as he and Devereaux made their way into the party. "I bet I do – you know – find out what's—"

"I know, Harper. I know."

Tara Madison had a pretty quick plan to get in, get the targeted contents, and get out. Wait for the party to really take off, have some men outside ready to create a diversion if need be. However, if the plan went according to scheme, when the time came there would be a pretty decent diversion going on from inside the party.

Getting past security cameras and security systems had never been a problem for Tara.

To her, B&E was nothing. Considering all the things that she had been through – the fights, the stabbings, the shootings, the scars – a Washington D.C., suburban security system was no problem, no matter how high-tech the homeowners were convinced that it was.

They were all the same, the security systems, and Tara knew it. This was not her first rodeo, but if everything went according to plan, it could very well be her most prosperous one – and her last.

The men and women had dispersed to their necessary places. It was just Kilpatrick and Madison left in the basement.

"Is this going to work?" asked Kilpatrick.

"Are you a good safecracker?"

"Well…yeah."

"Are you a *fast* safecracker?"

"I was told by a little bird that this particular safe is an AMSEC, LP series, composite, wall safe. If that's true, then there's no one faster."

"Then this is going to work."

"I don't know you."

"I don't know you either," Madison replied, "but it's not like we're here to make friends. Just here to make some money."

"Okay," Kilpatrick replied a bit nervously. He wasn't a big fan of doing jobs with total strangers. That's how he ended up doing time in the first place. "Do you think they're in place? The others? Time to go?"

Madison looked at her wristwatch. "Not quite yet."

The party had been going for about two hours, and Kinley Devereaux and Harper Rowe were having a blast. They were mingling with some of the most high-powered political figures the nation's capital had to offer.

Devereaux was smooth as always. At one point, earlier in the evening, he had found himself engaged in conversation with one of D.C.'s younger, more attractive, delegates.

"Did anyone ever tell you that you look like that actor Liev Schreiber?" she asked for no apparent reason.

"That's a compliment, right?"

"Oh," she smiled slyly, "that's definitely a compliment."

"Good. I didn't want to make you – *scream* – or anything."

The two laughed pleasantly before the young delegate leaned in and whispered into his ear, "Play your cards right, cowboy, and you just might."

However, for all the silver-tongued charm that Kinley Devereaux wielded, his partner, Harper Rowe – not so much.

"Harper Rowe," one senator said with a friendly southern accent as he shook the assassin's hand, "I hear you shoot people for a living."

"Now, Senator – Rawlings, is it? From Georgia?" Harper pulled his hand back. "What on earth would make you ask me a question like that?"

"Oh, I don't know. People talk; rumors abound."

To Harper, it sounded like the senator was drawing out the ending of almost every word he spoke. Perhaps, he thought to himself, that is why it was referred to as a southern drawl.

"Well, people are idiots, and you, Senator Rawlings, are an even bigger one if you listen to them."

Kinley, who was standing just a few feet away, felt the hair on the back of his neck stand up when the words from Harper's response made their way like a freight train into his tympanic membrane. Kin moved quickly to interrupt his friend's conversation before it got too out of hand. But he was too late, as Harper just kept sticking his foot further and further into his mouth.

"And just for the record, Senator: I don't shoot people for a living. I *kill* people – for a living."

And Devereaux swept in, "Forgive my friend, Senator. He's had a bit much to drink." Kinley was quick to usher his friend away. "Are you drunk, you dumb ass?"

"What?"

"What?" Devereaux asked incredulously. "Just move, Poptart."

"What did I do?"

"You're acting like a total jackass," Devereaux said as he

ushered his best friend out onto a balcony that was adjacent to the huge party room.

"Oh, I'm the jackass. And tell me, my good friend, why is that?"

"Will you keep your stinking mouth shut for one stinking minute?"

Harper Rowe put his hands up in the air and backed away from Kinley. "This is me keeping my mouth shut."

"Seriously, Harper. There may be people in there that know who we are, and there are a lot of people in there that think they know what we do, but – brass tacks, baby – if anybody even suggests that they even have a notion about us and what we do – redirect 'em, okay? – and just deny, deny, deny." Kinley was speaking in a harsh whisper. "Buddy, any way you slice it…we're top secret, and we don't say anything to anybody about what we do. You've been doing this long enough to know that."

"Not to change the subject, but – how do you feel?" Harper had a look on his face that was equal parts quizzical and happy.

"I'm pissed! That's how I feel."

"I'm drunk."

"Really?" Devereaux looked incredulously at Harp. "Well, now there's a stunning revelation," he said dryly. "For cryin' out loud, man. What if I hadn't been hanging around when I was? Were you just gonna give us both up to the good senator?"

"No." Harper still seemed a bit disconcerted by something besides Devereaux's antagonistic questions. He kept squinting his eyes and moving his head from side to side like he was trying to focus on a fly in the rain.

Kinley clapped his hands in front of his buddy's face. "Hey! You need to pay attention here—"

"I'm *drunk*," Harper said once again, this time as if he were stating an amazing fact to the whole world. He then looked at Kinley and shook his head, "Something's wrong, Kin."

"What are you talking about?"

"I'm drunk."

"So you've said. What is it exactly that you think is wrong? You drink copious amounts of alcohol and that's what happens."

"You've been drinking?"

"Two and a half beers since we got here. Well within my legal limit."

"I haven't had a drop."

"C'mere," Kinley was livid as he grabbed Harper by the collar and took a long, close-up look at his friend. "I need you to do me a favor. Come with me. Don't ask why – just do it." In unison the two men made their way to the balcony railing that overlooked the huge acreage that was Doug Hopkins' backyard.

"Somebody spunched the pike."

"Somebody spiked the punch?"

"Yeah, that's what I said," retorted Harper. "Somebody spiked the punch. That's all I've been drinking, but, honest to Pete, if I wasn't hanging on to you right now, I'd be lying down there on Hopkins' astrograss."

Devereaux and Rowe turned and leaned their backs against the balcony railing. They looked at every one that was on the large balcony, then peered in through the balcony doors, as everyone inside seemed to be hugging and kissing and dancing the night away.

"What kind of party did we get invited to, Harp?"

THE HEIST

The key to any good heist was to have an inside man. Tara Madison knew that she and her crew in the basement were not the first pieces of this chess game to be put in play. The first piece was Desmond Timms, an African-American con man that stole more money before 9:00 a.m. than most thieves stole all year. Today, Desmond had been put in charge of running the party for the Under Secretary of Defense, Douglas G. Hopkins.

Not so much put in charge, as conned his way into the position.

With all the hubbub and excitement that had been going on at the Hopkins' household, and with all the security protocols that had been put in place, it was pretty easy for Timms to get clearance. Nowadays, pretty much any moron that had half a brain about computers could make up an identity that was good enough to pass a standard three-tiered security background check. And Desmond Timms was certainly a far cry from a moron.

Timms had written his own computer clearance months ago when he first heard about the job. No one was looking to dig too deep into the party planner's background after the first three layers of him being him had checked out. Funny how the one guy they were just *certain* was on the up and up ended up being the person that would come back and bite them in the ass the most.

Still, Desmond Timms had such a professional manner about him that no one thought even once about him being a decent-sized pawn in the middle of a major U.S. conspiracy.

And that was the first mistake.

The second mistake was that no one bothered to check the punch or the food for any "added ingredients." The king's tasters had somehow been left off the guest list. Timms had brought his own little party favorites to the event. The first was a synthetic liquid that was basically a designer form of ecstasy.

Slipped into the punch bowl, the drug was colorless, tasteless, and odorless, and the high that it gave off was a very natural, very powerful high. It was like all the endorphins in your brain had kicked in and were taking you for an erotic ride in the clouds. It explained why there were so many people dancing on the dance floor in Hopkins' home. It also explained why people were standing so close to each other, and why perfect strangers were kissing and hugging for no apparent reason.

Timms did not limit his exploits to the punch bowl. He also had brought with him multiple tablets of the actual drug ecstasy, which he had ground into a fine powder. Since he was the party planner, it was his job to check all the food that was being served to make sure it was fit for the so-called kings and queens of Washington D.C. That gave him a chance to place just enough of the illegal powder into all the food that was being partaken of to get everybody "in the mood." So far everything was going according to plan.

"All right, Kilpatrick, get your things together. It's time for us to move."

Jason held up his hands and moved his fingers around. "These are the only things that I brought with me."

"Then here we go."

Tara led the duo out the back door of the basement and cautiously made her way to the front corner of the building. She stuck her com in her ear. "Is everybody in place? Kilpatrick and I are headed out and headed in."

"Roger that, Team Leader. Unit 2 in position."

"Copy that, Team Leader. Units 3 and 4 in position."

"Hey, Team Leader," Desmond Timms said happily from the kitchen. "Unit 1, and it's all good in here. Peoples are lovin' on one another like it was the end of the world. Still, I don't think it would be a bad idea to hit the front door with a little somethin' somethin' just to keep them off their toes."

"Roger that, Unit 1. I assure you the front door will be hit with a little something, something," Madison replied. "Moving in on target now. All units keep radio contact. Unit 2 get ready to hit the door."

"Oh, and Team Leader," came back Timms, "if you don't mind…let me know when you have what you need and are free and clear cuz I'll be on up outta here. This party's getting a little too rich for my blood. Ya dig?"

"Will do, Unit 1," Madison turned to Jason Kilpatrick and grabbed his hand. "Stay close to me, Kilpatrick. If we're going to be avoiding the security cameras then I don't need you straggling behind."

"I don't know, Kin," Harper said as he, too, was scanning the balcony and what he could see of the inside of the Hopkins home. "It looks like everybody's having a blast."

"A little too good of a blast," Devereaux responded.

"Oh, geez, here comes the highlight of the night. Kelly's walking this way." Kelly Campbell was the mission assigner and handler for both Devereaux and Rowe. She loved Kinley to death, but hated Harper with a passion. She made it a point to give the worst assignments that crossed her desk to him in hopes that, somehow, he would be killed in action. That's how much she hated him.

Still, despite her best attempts, Harper Rowe kept coming back successful, again and again and again.

To Kinley, she gave the cushiest of assignments, in the most heavenly of places. Waikiki, Paris, Sydney – Oh, how she loved Kinley Devereaux.

So, it was really odd when Kelly waltzed up to Harper Rowe, put her arms around his neck, and squealed, "Harr-perr – I have missed you."

Harper put his arms around her waist and squeezed tight as he turned his head toward his partner. He caught Kinley's glance and lipped, "What the—"

Kinley smiled and asked, "Convinced now?"

And it was just about that time that there was a bit of somethin' somethin' at the front door.

Unit 2, which was made up of two men, Lionel Akins and Jay Painter, and one woman, Sierra Gayle, wasted no time making its way up to the front entrance of Doug Hopkins' palatial home. They had been crouched down in the darkness for some time. At first they were hidden just outside of the security fence, behind some bushes and shrubs, out of sight of the cameras. Once darkness fell, they waited for a car to pull through the security gate. Then the trio moved into position and awaited instruction from Tara Madison.

Akins, Painter, and Gayle had been hiding for some forty minutes when they heard their earpieces crackle. "This is Madison. Unit 3 and Unit 4, are you in position?"

"Unit 3 here. Ready to go."

"Unit 4 here. Loaded and waiting."

"Unit 2, this is Madison. Kilpatrick and I are taking the house. Unit 2, hit the door. Unit 3, wait for my go."

Akins, Painter, and Gayle walked forcefully toward the front door of the house. At this point in the evening, most of the party guests had already arrived. The security men stationed at the front door walked passively toward the trio, holding up their hands. "Whoa, whoa, whoa, gang! Let's just hold up right there and pull out the invites."

Gayle pulled out the bottle of mace and sprayed it into the eyes of the security guards. Moments later, the very same men were being pummeled by Lionel Akins and Jay Painter.

"Unit 3, cut the power now!" Madison barked into her headset as she and Kilpatrick began ascending the wall of the Hopkins house. Using suction cup climbers, they made their way up like spidermen toward the targeted room.

As darkness enveloped Doug Hopkins' home and his entire neighborhood, Harper was quick to toss Kelly Campbell aside into Kinley Devereaux's arms.

"Looks like somethin's goin' on out front. I'll see ya there."

Kinley caught Kelly, and without missing a stride he set her upright like a doll against the outside balcony railing, then ran inside after his best friend.

"Yo, Harp! Don't do anything stupid!"

Unit 3 waited until they thought everyone's eyes had gotten used to the dark, and they were sure Tara Madison had breached the security cameras, then they cut the power back on. For just a few moments, everyone was blinded, and that was all they needed.

Unit 2 had made their way inside the Hopkins' mansion just as the lights came back on. Akins, Painter, and Gayle had drawn their weapons and were ready to shoot their way in, but the two guards at the bottom of the staircases had already drawn their guns.

When the lights came back on, both guards had no problem

emptying their clips into the three home intruders. Akins, Painter, and Gayle hit the floor lifelessly, just as the two staircase guards were sliding their next clips into their weapons. They left their posts and walked toward the dead trio that was once Unit 2. "I'm calling 9-1-1," the first guard said.

"I got you covered. Checkin' 'em for signs of life." As the two guards took care of business, they totally missed an inconspicuous Harper Rowe as he quietly sneaked behind them and made his way up one of the staircases. Kinley Devereaux was not far behind.

"Harper, what are you doing?" Devereaux practically fell down as he turned the corner to make his way up the stairs after his partner.

"Keep it down, Cisco," Harper hushed as he flighted the top of the stairs quickly and quietly. "Told you I'd get up here," he whispered. Harper hit the top of the staircase.

At this point, Madison had no problem popping the security wires on the outside window to the Hopkins home. If there was one thing Tara Madison had learned in all her days of criminality, it was this: the more a homeowner spent on outside security, the less they spent on inside security. Popping the upstairs window to the room they had targeted and then climbing inside, she and Jason were quick to move to the safe that was inside the room.

"Okay, Kilpatrick, let's make this fast. The party of louts downstairs won't wait forever."

Devereaux was a little too close in his pursuit of his partner, so when Harper stopped short at the top of the stairs, Kinley could not help but run up his back and knock him to the floor.

"Nice," Harper said as he rolled over on his back and popped back to his feet. "As if there wasn't enough noise downstairs—" Harper's head snapped to the side as he immediately stopped talking. He lifted his hand to silence anything that Kin might be getting ready to say. "I heard something," he whispered in the slightest of tones.

He started walking down an upstairs hallway.

"Harper!" Devereaux whispered harshly, only to be given the silent hand signal. He looked back down the staircase at the commotion on the first floor. He decided it was in his best interest to just stay upstairs for the time being and see what Harper was getting into.

But when he turned his head back to see where Harper was, he had disappeared. Devereaux looked up and down the hallway but all he saw was darkness. He took a moment to listen for any sounds that might give him a clue as to where his friend may have gone.

He heard a gunshot, a thud, some yelling, glass shattering, another gunshot, a familiar voice shouting "Kin, get your ass in here!"

"Harper?" he tried not to say too loud. He made his way toward the noises he had heard. It was dark. He put his hands up against the walls, hoping to find a lightswitch as he made his way down the black hallway.

Another muffled gunshot, and then thudded footsteps. He found his way to the room the noise was coming from just in time to peer through its doorway and see his partner perched in the window.

"Dude! Where ya been?"

Kinley flipped the lightswitch on. The bright lights made him squint and cock his head back like a rooster.

"Harper? What are you doing in the window?"

"Somebody was in here. They took something from that safe," Rowe pointed toward the safe. "*They* freakin' shot at me, so *I'm* going after *them*."

"Do you have a gun?"

"Do I ever?" Rowe shifted his body on the window's ledge. "See ya 'round downtown, partner."

"Harper, don't do—" Kinley cut his sentence short as he watched his buddy launch himself from the second-story window and down to the ground. "I swear I'm gonna kill you, Harp," Kinley whispered to himself.

He quickly made his way back down the hallway to the top of the stairs, but more trouble was heading up the stairs than had just jumped out the window.

Kin wasted no time returning to the room. He climbed into the same windowsill from which he had just seen Harper jump.

By now, with the power cut back on, the backyard, front yard, and side yards of the Hopkins home were completely lit up. As Devereaux perched himself in the window, he could see his partner climbing over the security wall. He heard footsteps coming down the hall toward him. Caught in a lose-lose situation, he took the same path as his best friend and leapt the two stories to the ground.

And Then Darkness

"Unit 4, Kilpatrick and I have a hot tail coming over the wall. Take that little S.O.B. out!" Tara and Jason were on a dead sprint toward her truck. She heard a clamor behind her. Just as she and Kilpatrick were mere yards from her truck, a single gunshot rang out from behind. Jason fell limply against the back of her legs. Tara turned around and saw him lying nearly dead on the ground. He reached up to her, "Don't leave me here. I can make it—" but his dying sentence was cut short by a bullet to the brain.

Tara looked up to see a darkly shadowed Harper Rowe running toward her from fifty yards away. Holding the contents from the Hopkins' safe in her left hand, she wasted no time as she secured it, drew her weapon from her hip, and fired at Harper in an attempt to slow his progress.

Milliseconds later she felt a blazing hot bullet graze her shoulder. Quickly giving up on Kilpatrick and all attempts to slow Harper, Madison tucked her weapon away and made a beeline to her truck. As soon as she swung open her driver's side door, she felt the weight of Harper Rowe land squarely on the back of her legs. Before she knew it, she was on the pavement with punishing blows from her assailant connecting over and over as he finally mounted her and put a gun into her face.

"You're hot," Rowe said as he pointed his weapon between Madison's eyes.

"And you're out of bullets, jerkwad," she replied as she reached down and grabbed her pistol. Suddenly, about two hundred yards from where they had just been, a massive exchange of gunfire took place. Both Rowe and Madison looked in the direction of the onslaught. None of the bullets seemed to be coming in their general direction. Rowe returned his attention to Madison.

"Am I? Because I just picked this up off of one of your dead guys back there."

"Yes," and she pointed her gun in Harper Rowe's face.

"Seems like we're having a moment here," the brash Rowe said. "I got my gun to you. You got your gun to me." He tightened his legs around her. "How's about we call it a night, you give me back what you took from that safe, and we both get away from the world of hurt that's back there from whence we came?"

"Not gonna happen, cowboy. Only way you get out of this alive is to drop your empty gun onto the pavement, get off me, and let me drive myself outta Dodge. Capiche?"

Harper was, at best, a novice at knowing the difference between how much a loaded gun and an empty gun should weigh. Still, he knew he could not let this woman get away with whatever was in her bag. He wondered if she really knew his gun was empty. Or was she bluffing?

"Your gun's empty," Madison said as if she were reading his mind. "If it wasn't, you wouldn't've tackled me."

"I was never much for gunplay, girlie. I like to do my killin' close up."

"Then you should've—"

A bullet whizzed between them, ricocheted off the pavement, and bounced away. Harper Rowe grabbed Madison's gun, but as he did, she flipped him off herself.

"Harper—" came a voice from far away.

Gun shots.

More bullets flew as Harper landed face first on the pavement and felt Madison's elbow in the back of his ribcage. She stood up and wasted no time climbing into her truck.

"Consider yourself lucky, jackass," she said as she gunned the engine.

"If I was lucky, you'd be making me a sandwich right now," Harper groaned as chunks of gravel and stone pounded his face while Tara Madison took off into the night. Then he saw darkness.

Dream State

"Harper—" came a voice from far away.

Harper opened his eyes and instinctively tried to take in his surroundings as quickly as he could. The pain in his face immediately kicked in.

"You with us, Harper?" a woman's voice asked.

He winced in pain and tried to talk. "Maybe."

"Just try to relax. We're taking you in."

Moments before he passed out again, Harper saw a woman's face and street lights streaming by, and smelled french fries.

GETAWAY

Tara Madison's lips were tight against the receiver of the payphone in the Baltimore/Washington International Airport.

"Are you at BWI?" crackled the voice on the other end of the line.

"I am."

"Then you know what to do."

Madison sighed and said, "There have been complications. I'm going to drop point #2."

"No. Don't do that," protested the man's voice in Tara's ear. "What kind of complications?"

"Too late," Tara said. "Already bought the ticket and am *boarding* now. See you there."

She hung up the phone, picked up her lone bag which contained the stolen item from the safe at Douglas Hopkins' house, and discreetly joined the line for the next flight out of Washington D.C. She looked around casually to be sure she was not being followed, then handed her ticket to the attendant.

"Thank you for flying with us today, Ms. Penders," the attendant said as she held the ticket under an ultraviolet light bulb, scanning for any discrepancies in the document. None were found.

"Here's your boarding pass," the attendant handed it back to Madison, "and have a wonderful flight."

"Thank you," Tara replied as she took the pass and boarded the plane that was headed out of the country. It was just a matter of minutes before she would be airborne and away from any danger. Once at her destination, she knew that the item she had gotten earlier that evening was going to make her very rich. Rich enough that she would never have to worry about anything ever again.

Another Scene in a Car

The traffic light clicked to yellow, and a small group of cars accelerated through the intersection before it turned red. One of the cars was a silver Dodge Charger. Two riders sat in the front seat; one rider sprawled out in the back seat.

The riders in the front of the car, Kelly Campbell and Kinley Devereaux, were quiet enough. They were hoping to get to their destination before their backseat passenger, Harper Rowe, came to cognisance. They sped quickly through the quiet early morning streets of Washington D.C.

"He's squirming around a lot back there. Sure you don't want to check on 'im?" Kelly asked Kinley.

"No," Kinley said, as he munched on some french fries. "Let's just wait till we get him to HQ. He's had a hard enough night. Besides, we're out here in the middle of the mean streets. People don't really give a crap if you got a sick passenger or not. I'd much rather just stay inside the car, if you don't mind."

Kelly accelerated the Charger. "Hang on," she said "they're calling." Devereaux looked over at her as she answered the call. "Hello," she said calmly as she sped through the dimly lit D.C. side streets. "Yes sir, I have them both with me."

Kinley slapped her on the arm and lipped, "Who is that?"

Kelly held up her index finger to shush her passenger. "Yes sir, I'm bringing them both in now. I'll have them to you in ten, sir." She disconnected and looked harshly at Devereaux. "Asshole!"

"What?" Kinley asked in bewilderment.

"That was my boss – your boss – and he's not happy."

"What's he gonna do?"

Campbell laid her head back against the headrest and straightened her arms as she maneuvered the steering wheel. "Better take your partner's lead and get some sleep. Gonna be a long night for the two of you."

"Well, what's that supposed to mean?" asked an exasperated Devereaux.

"I don't know what you two've stumbled into, but he's pissed, and he wants answers. And from everything I've experienced with him, that means one thing: a very long night. He's not going to let you guys up for air until he hears what he wants."

"I don't even know anything so how am I supposed to tell him what he wants to hear?" Devereaux exhaled disgustedly as he turned to look out the passenger side window. He had been looking forward to this night for some time – the party, the people, a chance to rub elbows – and not only was he not able to enjoy it like he had hoped, now it seemed that he was caught in the middle of some sort of government or domestic or international conspiracy. He slammed his hand against the dashboard in anger. "Unbelievable, Harper! Why'd you have to go up those stairs?"

When they pulled into the parking lot of the State building where their headquarters was based, military agents were waiting for them. Campbell and Devereaux cautiously got out of the car.

"What's going on here?" Kelly asked, somewhat perturbed.

"M'am, we need you and Mr. Devereaux to accompany us upstairs. Where's Mr. Rowe?"

"He's in the back of the car. Unconscious."

Without a moment's hesitation, one of the larger military men moved to the back door of the Charger, opened it up, and began pulling on Harper Rowe's motionless body.

"Whoa! What is *this* noise? I don't think so!" Devereaux went to move toward the agent but was immediately restrained by two others. He quickly put his hands up in the air. "Okay, okay. Take it easy with my buddy there."

"Don't worry, Mr. Devereaux, he's in good hands."

Kinley looked over at his boss and shook his head. It suddenly occurred to him how right she was. It *was* going to be a long night.

12

By Order of the President
of the United States

Harper Rowe was dragged into the room and slung down on the floor. The back of his head bounced on the tile floor as the rest of his body followed suit. The man that carried him into the room and tossed him carelessly onto its floor was soon met with the harsh reality of Kinley Devereaux's fist.

"Kinley," Kelly Campbell squealed, "calm down!"

"Pick 'im up!" Kin barked.

"And do what with him, sir?" the military man asked as he recoiled slightly, then stood at attention.

Taking stock of the room, Devereaux saw that there was not a single piece of furniture. Just an empty room with painted cinder block walls and a cold tile floor, dimly lit with fluorescent lights.

"Ah, I don't know," Kinley said, somewhat defeated. "Put 'im up against the wall – nicely, though."

"No," Harper suddenly spoke groggily. "I got it there, Portnoy."

"Harp, you all right?" Devereaux came over to his aid.

"I think so. Apparently Neanderthal man there knocked me conscious when he dropped me on my head." Harper looked around slowly as he slid himself up against the nearest wall. "Probably should've paid the extra three dollars for the rental insurance on this tux. Pretty sure the good people down at 'Johnny's Formal Attire and Muffler Shop' are gonna be thrilled when I try to get my deposit back on this thing."

Before Devereaux could answer, a middle aged man in a black suit walked into the room. "Everybody out," he ordered curtly. "Mr. Devereaux, Mr. Rowe, I need to speak with you directly."

Campbell stepped up to him. "Who are you? Where's Mr. Lange?"

"Kelly!" came a man's voice from the doorway. It was Gerald Lange, Kelly Campbell's boss. "As much as I'd like to tear these two a set of new assholes, this man is in charge here now."

"Sir, what is going on?" she asked fiercely.

"Kelly, this is officially out of our hands now. Let's go."

"But sir – "

"Now!" Lange barked.

Campbell glanced back at Devereaux. "Sorry, Kinley." She quickly left the room, pulling the door closed behind her.

By now Harper had made it to his feet. He was still rubbing the back of his head when he asked, "Do we get to know who you are?"

"My name is Aaron Templeton. I'm here by order of the President of the United States of America. Gentlemen, we currently find ourselves in an unbelievable crisis of national security, and right now – the two of you are all we've got. Sirs, your country needs you."

"Needs us to do what?" Devereaux asked in an Arnold Drummond *Whatchoo talkin' 'bout, Willis* tone of voice.

"Unfortunately, I'm not at liberty to say. There's a chopper on its way here now to take us to the Pentagon where, it's my understanding, you'll be debriefed and given further instructions."

"Debriefed on what exactly? What happened at the Under Secretary's house tonight?"

"To be honest, sirs, we're still gathering intel on exactly what happened. There are those who seem to think the two of you will be vital to that process."

"Well, those people gotta be on crack, Templeton. I mean, seriously, we gave a brief pursuit of the intruders, but I, for one, didn't see much more than some silhouettes and shadowy figures in the distance. It all happened so unbelievably fast." Devereaux put his hands up and shrugged his shoulders. He looked at his friend, "Did you see anything of any significance?"

Harper looked at his partner. He knew exactly what Kinley was doing, and he knew exactly what Kinley wanted *him* to do.

Lie.

Lie like a rug.

Lie like a con man at a liar's convention.

Lie, Harper, Lie!

Please lie to this man and tell him you didn't, couldn't, had no recollection of ever seeing anything that could be of assistance to anyone at the Pentagon about what happened at Doug Hopkins' house tonight.

Lie.

Kinley looked at his partner. He knew exactly what Harper was going to do, and he knew it was exactly what he did *not* want him to do.

"Mr. Rowe?" Templeton asked. "Did *you* see anything tonight at the Hopkins' estate that might be considered – *of any significance?*"

Harper looked at his buddy. He covered his face with his hands and slowly wiped away whatever blood had gathered on his visage. He spit on the floor, looked at Templeton, and said, "You bet your sweet life, I did."

"And...?"

"And what I have to say is probably best said at the Pentagon."

A few minutes later, Kinley and Harper found themselves on board a military escorted express flight straight to the Pentagon. A Huey with two pilots, two gunners at the doors and room for four – of which there were only two.

Harper Rowe. Kinley Devereaux

The duo sat quietly for the first few minutes of the ride, then Kinley put his arm around Harper's neck. "How's your face feel?"

"Like I just went twelve rounds with the champ, and he hit me with all twelve rounds, then reloaded and hit me with another twelve rounds."

"Looks like most of the bleeding's stopped. Maybe once we get where we're going they can patch you up a bit."

"Yeah, maybe," Harper winced as he touched the wounds on his face. "You need to back off, Harp," Devereaux sighed.

"And do what?"

"Just tell them you pursued, but in the end – you didn't see anything."

"Kinley, take a look around, dude. This isn't going away. We're on a million dollar helicopter with armed escorts on our way to the Pentagon. That was a well-planned attack on the Under Secretary's house tonight. I have to believe this is way bigger than you or I could possibly imagine. I'm not gonna lie and just sweep it under the proverbial rug." Harper was quiet for a moment and then, "I do have a couple questions for you, though."

"Like?"

"When I was chasing that woman away from the Under Secretary's house, I heard an inordinate amount of gunfire behind me at one point. What was that?"

"When I came over the security wall to see where you were, you were right behind her, man, but then came this collection of people with guns that were coming up behind you. As close as you were to her, they were going to take you out. So, I jumped off that security wall – and as mad as I was at you for going up those stairs, I still couldn't let you die. I guess I took the anger I had at you – out on them."

"Geez, dude. How many people did you kill?"

"Like – eight."

"Eight?"

"Maybe ten. I wasn't really counting when I ran past them. I saw that girl peel out in your face, and I just figured you could probably use my attention more than my stat sheet could." Devereaux stared for a moment at his friend. "I don't wanna do this, Harp."

"I'll leave you out, then. After all, I saw the woman. I was the one that walked in on the robbery, and I was the one that chased them down. Whatever the Pentagon wants, I'll make sure you're not caught up in it."

"There's just one problem."

"No, there's not a problem. I'll take care of this."

"Yes, there is, Harper. I saw them, too."

"Wait. What? When?"

Devereaux leaned back in his seat. "It was a man and a woman, right? That broke into the place?"

"Yeah."

"While you were in pursuit of them – I was in pursuit of you. I'm the one that killed the man, and I'm also the one that was firing away when the woman was getting ready to kill you. She got in a truck and peeled out in your face. By the time I got to you – you were out."

"Hmmm. I kinda remember that. Thanks, by the way."

Devereaux put his hand on Harper's knee. "I'm a selfish prick, but if you wanna do this"—Kinley shook his head in disbelief at what he was getting ready to say— "count me in."

"So, why the sudden change of heart?"

Devereaux shrugged. "It's like you said – this could be something really big. You think I'm gonna leave you on your own to run this thing into the ground like Wile E. Coyote on an ACME rocket?"

Rowe slapped his partner on his arm and smiled, "Just can't let me have my moment of glory, can you?"

Devereaux showed a glimmer of a smile and said, "Not in this lifetime."

New and Fun Things to Do

It was no secret that the Pentagon was a very sophisticated building by design – full of hidden chambers and intricate hallways – and built in concentric rings. There were five floors above ground, and two floors below. The basement was built like a bomb shelter to the stars – and the President. Each ring was marked "A" through "E," with "F" and "G" being the basement rings. It was also designed so that you could walk from any two points of the Pentagon within eight minutes.

Now, a blindfolded Harper Rowe and Kinley Devereaux had no idea of what floor they were on or what direction they were headed.

"Harp, you still with me?"

"Of course. Can't you tell by the smell of my Hai Karate?"

"I thought that was dog vomit, but, yeah, now that ya mention it—"

One of the armed guards that was taking them to their destination snapped, "Sirs, be quiet. We're almost to your destination."

Harper listened closely to the direction of the guard's voice. "Sorry, bud, I didn't hear what ya said there."

"Sir, I asked you to be please be quiet."

Harper zoned in on just where the guard was in relation to his position. Rowe clenched his fist and was ready to blindly fire away.

"Harp, don't," Devereaux said, reading his friend's mind. "Let's just get to where they want to take us and find out what's going on. Now, more than ever, is not the time for your shenanigans."

Harper unclenched his fists. "I'm just a little claustrophobic with these blindfolds on. Makes me a little on edge, is all."

The guards soon turned Kinley and Harper over to the Pentagon security guards, who took the two assassins on another fifteen-minute walk, then put them into an office and left them there, alone.

Once they heard the door shut and had listened carefully to make sure there was no one else in the room, Kinley said, "What office do you think we're in?"

"Did you take your blindfold off yet?"

"No. You?"

"Duh, dreamboat, if I had taken my blindfold off, why would I be asking you if you had taken *your* blindfold off?"

"I'm too afraid to take my blindfold off. I'm too afraid that I'll be staring at a firing squad, and there will be a little Asian man standing there with one of those clove cigarettes."

"I know, right? Clove cigarettes totally suck. I think I'd rather just go ahead and get shot right then and there than to have to suffer the agony of having to suck on a clove cigarette for five minutes."

Neither man had taken off his blindfold, so they were both surprised when they heard the voice of another. "It's okay, men. I'll vouch for both of you on this one."

"Dad? Is that you?" Harper asked mockingly. He and Kinley removed their blindfolds to see that they were in yet another office. This time, however, it was well lit, well furnished, and there were six well-dressed individuals sitting around a long boardroom table. "Kinda late for a board meeting, ain't it?" Harper asked no one in particular.

"Gentlemen, my name is General David Higgins. The people sitting around the table are—"

"It's not important, General. Are you in charge here?" Devereaux asked.

"General Higgins," Harper Rowe said as he plopped down in one of the open chairs at the boardroom table, "you're obviously in charge here. If you weren't—" Harper leaned back in his chair and touched the man that was adjacent to him. "How ya doing, pal?" Before the man or anyone else at the table could say anything, Harper leaned forward and said to General Higgins, "If you weren't, you wouldn't be standing at the head of the class getting ready to give roll call."

"As I was getting ready to say," continued the general, "the people sitting around the table are here strictly on a functional basis."

Harper raised his hand. "Can I ask a question?"

"By all means, Mr. Rowe," the general conceded.

"When you say 'functional basis,' does that mean they're here because it was their goods that got stolen tonight? Because I've heard the term 'functional basis' used before, and I'm pretty sure that's what it means."

"They're here to make sure I do my job correctly, and part of my job is making sure that information is kept on a need-to-know basis, Mr. Rowe."

"So, in other words, you're not going to tell me why they're here, are you?"

"That is correct, sir."

"Are you gonna tell us why *we're* here?" Kinley asked.

"Now *that*, I can tell you." Higgins looked at Devereaux and Rowe sternly. "Boys, the party at the Under Secretary's house tonight was a thing that political nightmares are made of. There were items there that weren't supposed to be there. The security was for shit. People that knew too much got away with a pretty well-staged robbery, and then there's the two of you, who crawled right smack into the middle of it all." The general pointed to the other empty chair at the table. "Have a seat, Mr. Devereaux."

Kinley took a quick scan of those around the table, then at his partner, before he reluctantly sat down. He looked back at Higgins and nodded.

"Let me start by asking the both of you what you know or saw that's pertinent to tonight's robbery."

"I saw the robbers," Harper spoke up. "Saw both of them, by accident, to be sure, but yeah, I saw both of them."

"Enough to make an identity?"

"No. Not at first. I mean, it was crazy, General Higgins. They were shooting at me, my partner came up behind me, the robbers jumped out the window, and then I went after them."

"Did you see what it was that they removed from Under Secretary Hopkins' house?"

"I was in pursuit of them," Harper emphasized. "It was a man and a woman. The man got shot and fell to the ground so I went after the woman. It was clear to me that she was carrying what was stolen or else she would have gone back and retrieved it off the dead guy – and I went after her to try to get it back. I engaged the woman, we struggled, but she got the best of me. I thought she was going to kill me, but then there was some gunfire, and she just left me laying. Got into her truck and took off." Harper gently touched his sore face. "I think I still got some of the rubble in my head."

General Higgins seemed to dismiss Harper Rowe's story as he turned to Devereaux. "And what did you see, Mr. Devereaux?"

"Like the kid said, General," Kinley began, "it was dark in the room where the man and woman hit the safe. Harp went out the window. I was gonna head back downstairs but, by that time, there was way too much traffic. I went out the same window Harper did. I saw him go over the security fence in pursuit, so I went right after him."

"And at any point," Higgins interrupted, "did it occur to you to–I don't know–stop and call for assistance or backup?" The general had a smug look on his face.

"I don't know you, general," Devereaux said somewhat disgustedly, "and I'm pretty sure you don't know who we are, but if you did, you'd know"—he looked at Harper, then back at General Higgins— "we don't have *backup*."

Devereaux cleared his throat and did not wait for General Higgins to respond. "As I was saying, I saw my partner go over the fence, and even though it took me a bit, I took the wall as well and continued my pursuit. Upon landing on the other side of the wall, I saw a small group of armed militants pursuing my partner."

"And what did you do?"

"The only thing I could do, General. I pursued."

"Go on—"

"Well, there were a lot of them, in a two by two formation. I grabbed one by the collar and slammed him down, popped him in the nose, and killed him. His side buddy turned around and drew his weapon on me, but by that time, I had the dead man's weapon. I pulled the dead guy up in front of me as a shield and then fired two rounds through his armpit. As you well know, General, nothing better than the human body to make a great silencer." Devereaux took a breath and then went off again. "The front group went off in pursuit of Harper. They had no idea what had happened behind them, so then I took all of them out from behind–yeah."

"That is almost poetic," Harper said as he lifted his left hand, "Up top."

Without looking at Harper or Harper's hand, Kinley continued talking as he went "up top" to his friend. "I continued my pursuit after the man and woman and Harper. I had a good angle at the dude that was with the woman. I, however, did not have a good angle at the woman as Harper was right up on her."

Devereaux looked around the long table that he and Harper were sitting at. "Umm, can I get some water before I go on?"

General Higgins walked around to the side of the table where a pitcher of water was sitting. He grabbed it and hurled it at Devereaux, hitting him right in the chest. "There's your water, Mr. Devereaux!"

"Whoa." Harper stood up. "Hey, man. That's not cool."

"Sit down!" Higgins ordered Harper. "You two have no idea how much damage you've caused this country tonight."

Harper Rowe sat back down, but said indignantly, "You must be on crack, General. We – me and Kin – we were the ones trying to get the bad guys. Don't go throwing water pitchers or whatever at us just because we were trying to help."

General Higgins walked back around the table and straight up to Kinley and Harper. "You didn't help. Okay?" Higgins grabbed the duo by their collars. "We set the perfect trap, you idiots! We had so many men undercover that you'd have to sneeze just to see the surface! That woman that broke into Hopkins' house and into his safe – she was our target!"

"We didn't know that," Harper argued.

Devereaux stood up from his chair and pushed the general away. "Back up, okay? Just back it on up, General."

"Or what? You going to ruin another assignment?"

"Or we won't tell you a stinkin' thing."

"That group of men you killed, Mr. Devereaux, the group that you thought were chasing your partner, they were ours. And the man that was with the woman, he was ours, too. But before he had a chance to report back to us, you effin-A killed him. And not only did our target get away, but they were able to steal what may be one of the most important pieces of information in the history of this country."

"Oh, please don't tell me they got the screenplay to *History of the World, Part I.*

I could never forgive myself," Rowe said in his usual slack-jawed manner.

"Harper!" Kinley hissed. "Zip it!"

Finally, someone from the opposite end of the table spoke up, "Gentlemen, my name is Steve Robbins. I work for Homeland Security." Robbins had a slight British accent, barely noticeable when he talked.

"Really?" Harper spoke up. "I didn't know they let guys from South East Wales work for Homeland."

Robbins laughed. "Very good, Mr. Rowe. You know your dialects quite well. Ever spent any time in Monmouthshire?"

"I've always considered myself a bit of a linguist. And – yes. Yes, a couple of years ago. Beautiful view of the stars from Monmouthshire. They've got the clearest skies in all the Kingdom."

Kinley smiled. For as long as he had known Harper, he was still amazed how the guy could go from class clown to valedictorian in a matter of seconds.

"Well, you see, Mr. Rowe, I'm retired Interpol, and a few months after I did that, I received a gracious invitation from your President asking me to be a consultant for U.S. Homeland Security. My wife had passed on a couple years before, you see, and I found myself with just a tremendous amount of time on my hands, so I obligingly accepted."

"Well, I'm sorry to hear about your wife. Nothing worse than losing someone you love way too early."

And suddenly, it was like there was no one else in the room except for Robbins and Harper Rowe.

"Thank you, Mr. Rowe. Your sympathy seems truly sincere."

"I assure you it is, sir, but sympathies aside, now that you have mentioned dialects, the woman we were chasing talked to me tonight."

"And?"

"Well, she was actually just yelling at me a lot, but I still did get a pretty decent read on where she was from." Harper closed his eyes, trying to think back. "Vancouver," he said hesitantly, "by way of Toronto."

"What else?" Higgins barked. "What else do you remember?"

"She was a little shorter than me, shorter black hair, and a tight face. I'm guessing anywhere from 25 – 28 years old. Thin, and was wearing one of those black faux-leather robber catsuits. That's about all I can remember."

Harper disregarded Higgins for the time being and talked back to Robbins. "So, who are we looking at here? Who'd we save from the clutches of the United States justice system tonight?"

"Truth be told, Mr. Harper, we're not very sure about that." At this point, Steve Robbins, retired Interpol, grabbed a pitcher of water and poured himself a glass. He took a quick sip. "One of the few things we've been able to gather was that our prey went by the name 'Black Ice' – hard to see, and usually too late upon which to react when encountered."

"Did you know Black Ice was a woman – and white?"

"No, and no."

"Do you know what it was that she took from the Under Secretary's safe?"

About that time, General Higgins stood to his feet and said, "Don't answer that, Mr. Robbins. That information is on a need-to-know basis."

Kinley stood up, wet clothes and all, took the empty water pitcher and fired it back at General Higgins. "Well, tell us what we need to know, ya dumb dick!"

Higgins was irate. "Fine. You two wanna know what you're doing here? You blew this investigation. Now you get to fix it."

"Whoa." Devereaux started. "So, by 'fix it,' you mean—"

"You and your partner, Mr. Rowe, get to find Black Ice, find out who knows about what she stole, and kill all of them. Not to mention, return the stolen contents safely to U.S. government hands."

"Look, General, I'm not sure what you know about us, but we're not the secret agent-spy types. I mean, yeah—"

"I know who you are, and I know what you do," said Higgins cutting him off. "You're a couple of stone cold killers for the NSA, CIA, DTTF, or whoever it is that will take a chance on you, but I don't really give a rat's ass. My orders are to give you two morons all the help you need to find Black Ice, kill her, and get those contents back. Any questions?" Higgins thought he was being nice to them, considering he was very much wanting to change their sexuality.

Harper raised his hand and spoke at the same time, "Yes, General Higgins, I was wondering – could I go home and change? I've been in this rental tux all night, and, did I mention it was a rental?"

"Like twice in the last three seconds, ass pie," Devereaux said in disgust, not so much at his friend, but just in general.

"No need to worry, boys, I've already taken care of that. I sent some agents to your respective homes to get you an extra bag of clothes."

Harper winced, "Um, general, I just recently moved. You *did* send them to the right address, didn't you?"

"What? You don't live in Delta anymore?"

Harper buried his head in his hands and mumbled, "I moved to White Marsh, jackass."

"Sorry, Mr. Rowe. Hope you like that rental tux. It's done pretty good for you so far tonight." General Higgins laughed inappropriately. "At least Devereaux here will have a fresh set of BVD's."

"I would just like to say that whoever's in charge of HR around here is gonna get my foot up their bum as soon as I get back from taking care of catsuit woman."

"Don't worry, Flash, you can wear some of my stuff."

"Yeah, Kin, but you're three inches shorter than me."

"But I'm mostly legs. The pants will be fine."

"That's cool, but the shirts will look like a crop top, dude." Suddenly, a young woman in a tight black skirt and button-down white blouse strolled into the room and up to General Higgins. She handed him a manila folder and walked out as quickly as she had walked in.

Devereaux looked at Harper, and the general looked at the manila folder. He slammed it down on the table. "Either of you boys ever do wetwork in Mexico City?"

"Not a lot," said Devereaux.

"Not that I'd ever admit," chimed Rowe.

General Higgins slid the manila folder across the desk toward the two assassins. "In that case, this particular job should be filled with new and fun things to do."

14

Change Up

Over the next 15 minutes several people walked in and out of the Pentagon boardroom – some talked to General Higgins, and some to the members around the boardroom table.

Kinley and Harper had left the room because, number one, priority-class secrets were being discussed, and number two, the agent that had been sent to Kinley Devereaux's apartment had returned with some clothes for the assassins. The two friends found themselves in a different office and, for the first time since they had been flown into the Pentagon, they had a free moment to speak between themselves. "When's the last time you were in Mexico City?" Harper asked Kin.

"Nine months ago. You?"

"Two and a half weeks ago. I hate that place – it sucks the big, bald weenie."

"Not my favorite place either," Devereaux said as he tossed Harper a pair of black pants. "Try those on. They're 34 waist."

"Do I look like I freakin' care about the waist size? How *long* are we looking at here?"

"Should be 32 long."

Harper stripped out of his tuxedo pants and lay down on his back, bent his legs, slid Kinley's pants over his feet up to his hips, jumped back up, pulled them up snug, and buttoned them. "Yeah," he said walking around back and forth, "these feel good. Nice."

"What the good, green earth was that?" Kinley asked.

"What?"

"That little production you just did there – lying down on the floor, putting on the pants and jumping up like you're some kind of kung fu artist."

"What can I say? I'm not like everybody else. I put my pants on *two legs* at a time."

Devereaux tossed him a t-shirt. "Try that on. It doesn't say 'I'm A Big Moron' on it, but it should."

Harper took off his tuxedo jacket, balled it up and threw it against the wall. "I hate Mexico City." He took off the frilly white tuxedo shirt and threw it over his head. "Yet, here we go again – into Mexico City." He pulled Devereaux's t-shirt over his head and down across his torso. "This looks outlandishly silly."

Kinley tried not to laugh at how tight and small his t-shirt was on Harper. "Oh, man, you look like a bad Ab-Buster commercial."

"At least, it's cotton."

Devereaux finally let his laughter out. He shook his head from side to side. "We are so screwed. What are we gonna do here, boss?"

Stretching out the t-shirt, Harper looked like a fly trying to escape from flypaper. Every time he pulled it away, it snapped back like a rubber band. He stopped a moment and said, "Well, it sounds like they're giving us the 'okay' to do what we do best, which is kill."

"Yeah, but to get to that point, we're gonna have to do some things that we've never had to do before. I'm a little unnerved by that." Kinley put on his own shirt, a light blue button-down Oxford. "Actually, a *lot* unnerved."

Harper returned to stretching the t-shirt. After several more tries he pulled it off and tossed it back to Kinley. "Forget that. I can't even break wind in that shirt, it's so small." As he walked over and picked up his tuxedo shirt, he said, "Higgins said they were going to give us all the help we needed. Still – you'd think if this was so dag-blasted important they would've gotten some retrieval specialists. I get the feeling the priority on this mission is wiping out anyone that has even a scosche of an inkling about any of this."

"Then why not get Seal Team Six or a group of erasers like them?"

Harper flapped his tux shirt into the air like an Amish woman flapping the crumbs out of a table cloth. "Because Seal Team Six and the like – they're the Michael Jacksons of the tactical world – they'll bring way too much attention to this situation. No, buddy, the gov'n'ment wants this, and everyone involved in it, to be put to death quickly, quietly, and without incident or accident."

"Is that up to – or including us, Harper?"

Rowe donned the tuxedo shirt once again and buttoned it up. "This looks okay, right?"

Kinley shook his head. "You look like a bad Leif Garrett impersonator."

WHAT PRETTY GIRLS DO

This early in the morning, the airport in Mexico City was not very busy. So when Tara Madison deplaned, there was no one there to meet her.

There was no one there to meet anybody.

Tara checked the clocks as she made her way through the deathly quiet airport. Whatever sounds there were came from announcements over the loudspeaker system giving departure and arrival times. It was 4:25 a.m. She was not headed for baggage claim because the only piece of luggage she was carrying was what she had stolen earlier back in the states.

Earlier. What was now, officially, yesterday.

Tara did not really care about the fact that yesterday had turned into today, nor did she care about the fact that the airport was practically hollow of human activity. What she did care about was meeting up with the man that had hired her. Meeting up with him and getting paid.

She walked outside the airport and onto the causeway and flagged down a green taxi. She climbed in.

"*A donde?*" the driver asked.

"*Hotel Habita, por favor.*"

"Oh, *Hotel Habita! Muy bueno. Muy bueno!*"

"*Sí, muy bueno,*" Madison agreed. "*Cuánto tiempo?*"

"*Quince minutos. Aproximadamente.*"

"*Vamonos, por favor. Vamonos.*"

"*Sí, sí!*" The driver floored the gas and the little green taxi took off toward the Hotel Habita.

*   *   *

Kinley and Harper walked back into the room where General Higgins and the information roundtable were all settled.

"Higgie, baby!" Harper said to the general. "We're back and ready for action."

General Higgins looked expressionlessly at Devereaux, but when he looked at Harper a scowl crossed his face. "And just what in the world is that outfit?"

"If I thought I was here for a fashion show, General Higgins, I'd be wearing your ass for a cummerbund." Harper looked around at the table's occupants. "Kinley and I are ready for our orders, sirs."

"I'm going to drive you to a private jet," Higgins said. "From there you'll be flown to Mexico City where you'll be met by a driver that will take you into to the city to one of the DEA flophouses that we control. You'll await further orders there."

"And when will we be given the necessary weapons to carry out our mission, sir?" Devereaux asked.

"Upon boarding the jet, the two of you will be given sidearms. Once you're taken to the flophouse, you'll be given the necessary weapons to carry out your assignment." Higgins looked at the two men. "Any questions?"

"I guess not," Devereaux said.

"Actually, I do have one," Rowe said as he made his way toward the far end of the boardroom table.

Higgins started to go after him, but Kinley cut him off. "Don't. Don't do that." Harper made his way to where Steve Robbins was sitting, picked the Brit up out of his seat by way of his collar, slammed him up against an adjacent wall, put his forehead up tight to Robbins' forehead, and asked in a harsh whisper, "Just how expendable are we on this, sir?"

Robbins blinked several times in fear before saying, "Like a trash bag, I'd have to say. I'm sorry, Mr. Rowe."

Harper released his grasp and pulled his head back. "Don't be. I'll see ya 'round downtown, Mr. Robbins."

*   *   *

The green taxi pulled into the Hotel Habita. Tara Madison paid the driver and stepped out into the early morning air. As the taxi pulled away, she looked up and down the street to be sure she had not been followed. Confident that she was on her own, she approached the front desk clerk easily, drawing no more attention to herself than necessary. Once she had caught the eye of the clerk, she smiled a beautiful smile.

"*Bueno.*"

"*Bueno, señorita,*" he replied, returning an equally impressive smile.

"*Habla Inglés?*" she asked politely.

"Of course," he replied, certainly smitten with her beauty.

"I'm expected in Room 219, Mr. Rubello's room. Could you please call up and let him know I'm here?"

The clerk smiled bashfully. "Yes. One second. I can certainly do that for you."

"*Gracias.*"

Madison stepped back from the counter, preparing for a quick getaway just in case the little perv of a front desk clerk did not get the answer from Paul Rubello that she was expecting. Her demeanor tightened as the clerk hung up the phone.

"Ma'am," he said looking at her.

"Yes?" she hesitantly stepped back up to the counter.

"The elevators are that way," he pointed to his left. "Mr. Rubello is expecting you."

Tara reached into her pocket for a few loose bills and set them on the counter in front of the clerk. "*Gracias*." She gave the clerk a knowing look, put her finger to her lips, smiled and said, "We don't want to be disturbed."

She made her way to the elevator, punched the up arrow, and waited patiently for the doors to open. As they did, she looked around one more time to be sure she was alone. Convinced that she was, she stepped through the doors and hit the button for the second floor.

When the elevator car came to a stop – just before the doors opened – Madison quickly reached into the front of her waistband to retrieve a two inch Blackhawk 5-shot pistol. She hid it behind the big belt buckle in front of her waistband as the elevator doors opened. Just as she expected, Paul Rubello was there to greet her.

"It's good to see you again, my friend."

Tara brought her hand around and gregariously shook Rubello's hand. "Good to see you, Paul. Sorry for the last minute change of plans."

Rubello greeted her warmly. "Let's go to my room. I don't like to do business in the hallway." He smiled, then quickly turned to lead her toward room 219.

Paul Rubello was two parts Kevin Costner, two parts Michael Phelps, and three parts The Devil. Older, but handsome with an athletic physique, an aura of pure evil, and a voice irritatingly similar to Ricardo Montalbán's. As she followed him to room 219, Madison reached under her shirt to make sure the safety on her pistol was set to *off*.

"Here we are," Rubello stopped and opened the hotel room door. "After you," he said congenially as he let Tara into the hotel room.

It was a nice room. The cab driver was not kidding – it was indeed *muy bueno*. To the right was a magnificent bathroom that contained both an eight-person hot tub, a whirlpool built for two, and a shower stall with a padded bench and two shower heads. On the opposite side of the bathroom was a triple sink and an entire wall that was nothing but mirrors. To the right, the room opened up into a sunken living room with a love seat, two recliners, and a magnificent couch that looked to be fit for only the most royal of hosts. Central to it all was a theatre screen television that hung from the ceiling – the projector built into the opposing wall.

On the far side of the sunken living room, three steps led up to two sliding doors. Behind the doors was a bedroom that contained a king-sized bed that looked like it was built for angels to sleep on. To the right was yet another hot tub – heart-shaped – and to the left was a door that led to a small five-person sauna.

And peppered amongst it all were five bodyguards, black suits and all.

"Wow," Madison said as she strolled into the room, somewhat star-struck. "This place is amazing." She looked at Rubello. "But, at the same time, I hope you don't think we're going to use any of this stuff."

"Of course not," he smiled innocently. "Do you have any weapons to declare?"

"Paul. Please. You know me better than that."

"Then pardon me for running a wand over your person. Just business, my dear."

"By all means," Madison said as she held up her arms.

One of the well-dressed bodyguards stepped over to Madison and ran the magnetic wand up and down her body. Across her arms, down her back, the outside of her legs, back up the inside of her legs, across her torso – beep. beep. beep.

Madison did not hesitate to lift her shirt to reveal a Texas-shaped belt buckle. "Ta-da!"

Neither the bodyguard nor Paul Rubello bothered to look past her big belt buckle to see the small bulge behind it which hid the 5-shot Blackhawk tucked just out of sight.

"I apologize for the inconvenience, but the security and the entourage is for my safety."

"Really?" Madison asked, looking bewildered. "Why?"

"This is serious business we do here, hon. Scary, unsettling, full of doubt, but I want you to know that Paul Rubello is a straight-up businessman that treats his people like movie stars. I want you to do some business with me, make some money, then enjoy this place. It's yours till Wednesday morning."

"No kidding?"

"No kidding, hon."

Tara smiled. "Well, I do like the big mirrors. And I absolutely love hot tubs. Not to mention, I have been up for awhile so that bed – oh my goodness."

"Exactly, babe. That's what I'm saying. You have gone above and beyond, sweetie," Rubello said as he walked into the room. "This – is all yours."

"So, where's my money?"

Rubello started to chuckle and with his thick Spanish accent said, "Okay. It's okay. I understand that you are anxious for your big payday. After all, you've been through hell."

"Got that right, I have."

"I just need to see the merchandise. I mean, you're a business-woman. Obviously, you understand that before I give you a quarter of a million dollars, I am gonna have to lay eyes on the product being delivered."

Tara walked down into the sunken in living room, removed a thumb drive from her front pants pocket, and slung it onto the dreamy couch. "There ya go, cowboy. Everything to make your dreams come true."

Rubello reached for the thumb drive just about the time Madison pulled the Blackhawk from the behind her Texas-sized belt buckle and shoved it into his temple. "Just one small change, Paul."

"Whoa, whoa, whoa," Rubello said as he stood up and put his hands in the air. "What's the problem here?"

"The price, Paul."

Rubello's bodyguards stepped forward as they pulled automatic weapons and trained them on Madison.

"Back off, boys. One false move, and your boss buys it – then I use his body as a human shield while I put you down one by one."

One of the bodyguards stepped forward to shoot her, but before he could pull the trigger, Madison sent a bullet through the front of his forehead. No sooner did his dead body hit the floor than Madison put the gun back to Paul Rubello's head. "Who's next, ass clowns? I got all night."

Rubello put on his best confused face, "Baby, we can work this out. No need—"

"Can and will," she said cutting him off. "Now, tell them to get out of here, or this ends right now." She positioned herself behind Rubello where none of the remaining bodyguards could get a shot at her.

"Look, we can work—" Rubello was cut off by Madison firing a bullet into another bodyguard. Two down, three to go.

"You're next, jackass," she whispered into Rubello's ear. "Tell them to leave, or it's over for you, right here, right now."

"Get out!" he yelled at the three remaining gunmen. "Get out and take them with you." Rubello pointed at the two dead men on the floor. "Out! Now!"

"No." Madison said harshly. "Put down your weapons." She pointed her gun at them again. The three men lowered their weapons and within seconds she fired the final three shots from her Blackhawk and assassinated the last three bodyguards.

"Now this is cozy, huh, Paul?"

"Yeah, yeah it is," he stammered. "Are you going to kill me?" Tara threw her empty gun onto the rug. "Yes, Paul. Yes, I am."

"Why?" he asked, almost crying.

"Because – it was a long flight down here, and I checked some things out, and it suddenly occurred to me just how bad you were screwing me on this deal."

"No – no," Rubello started peeing his pants.

"You wanna live through this, Paul?"

"Yes, yes. Please, just tell me what you want, and it's yours, I swear."

"Who's setting up the meeting with the buyers?"

"What?"

Madison tightened her grip on Rubello's neck. "Stop screwing around, Paul," she hissed. "Who's setting up the meeting with the buyers that are going to buy the contents of the Under Secretary's safe? This is your last chance. Tell me what I want to know."

"Desmond. Desmond Timms. He's setting everything up. The time, the place, the buyers."

"There now. Was that so difficult?"

"No," he answered feebly. "Are you going to let me go? You said you would."

"Well, I thought it over, and – no."

Rubello, knowing what was coming next, tried to say a quick prayer. He got as far as "Mother Mary" before he heard his neckbones crack as Madison swiftly turned his head 180 degrees.

Tara Madison was not going to waste much time searching the hotel room for the money Rubello had brought to pay her. After all, she knew there was a much bigger payday awaiting her. However, it was no surprise to find that Rubello had hidden the money in the headboard of the king-sized bed. It was the first place she looked. *Stupid perv*. She snatched the money, went back to the living room couch for the thumb drive, then it was out of the hotel room and into the big time.

She grabbed the 'Do Not Disturb' sign and placed it on the outside doorknob, then made her escape down the hotel's back stairwell.

It would be another several hours before anyone knew what she had done. By then, she'd be well on her way to being richer than she could have ever imagined.

Takeoff

As the morning skies began to lighten, Harper and Kinley sat in the back seat of a black sedan as General Higgins sped without regard for human life toward the private runway where a jet was fueled and ready to take the two assassins down to Mexico City.

"Umm, General?"

"Yes?" he asked without taking his eyes off the road or slowing down.

"Do you really want us to make it to Mexico City, boss? Or was that just a big show to get us in your car and kill us all?" Harper and Kinley were sliding all over the backseat while the car sped crazily toward their destination. "Cos we can get out and walk."

"You boys are fine."

"Then I got a question, General," Devereaux said as he grasped the back of General Higgins' driver's seat and righted himself.

"Fire away, son."

"We're getting flown into Mexico City – what are we supposed to do next?"

"We got a DEA flophouse on the west side of the city. We got a team there – they're the ones that are giving us the information we have so far on Black Ice – they will be waiting for you when your plane lands. Once you're on the ground and with them, they'll be running the operation."

"And they'll get us out? Or are we just supposed to sneak back across the border with the Barrio Brothers?"

"With what you're retrieving for your government, boys,"— Higgins paused for dramatic effect— "we'd pull you out with a towbar and chain if we had to."

Harper Rowe righted himself by hanging onto the passenger side back door. He spoke up. "You're not that bright, are ya, General?"

"Meaning?"

"Meaning – we pull this off – then where do we go? Who do we report to? When we get back the stolen documents, do we just drop 'em in the mail?"

Higgins laughed heartily. Kinley and Harper feigned hearty laughter in return. "Don't worry, fellas." Higgins snickered. "You do your job – we'll do ours." Higgins slowed the car down and took a right on a one-lane access road that headed east, directly into the rising sun.

Kinley looked at Harper and asked quietly, "What in the Sam Hill does that mean?"

"General, is it too late to back out of this?"

"Boys, I got a Desert Eagle in a shoulder holster under my left arm. It's fully loaded, and I wouldn't think twice about emptying its contents into both of your heads. So, yeah, it's way too late for either of you to pull the plug on this mission."

Harper was silent. Kinley ran his hands through his hair. The two friends looked at each other. "General, I can't wait to tell my friends that I know who you are," Harper said excitedly.

Finally, the plane – the private jet – came into sight. Higgins pulled up to within about 50 yards of the craft. "There ya go, boys. Your bird awaits you."

"Can you pop the trunk, General?" Devereaux asked. "I got a bag in the back."

"No problem, champ," Higgins said as he pushed a button under the dash and opened the trunk.

Devereaux opened his back door and hopped out while Harper stayed in the back seat. Harper waited till his cohort had shut the door, and then he leaned forward and said quietly to Higgins, "Hey, give me your Desert Eagle."

"What?"

"Give me your Desert Eagle," Harper repeated.

"Shouldn't you be getting *your* bags out of the back, too?"

"No," Harper said somewhat disgustedly. "Apparently, HR can't pull their heads out of their collective asses with a pair of tweezers, so I didn't get a bag. Do you think I'd really be wearing this ridiculous shirt if I had an alternative?"

"You're right. That's a horrible shirt, but you're still not getting my gun."

"Eh," Harper shrugged, "it was worth a shot. See ya 'round downtown, General," and Harper opened and slid out of the passenger side door.

The private jet was nice. Harper and Kinley sat across from each other, giving the inside of the craft a couple of good side-to-side glances. The seats were big and soft and covered in fine leather, positioned at a ninety-degree angle against the wall on the pilot's side of the plane. There was a full-sized refrigerator built into the opposite wall, a large screen television just over Kinley's shoulder on the reverse side of the back wall of the cockpit. The middle aisle seemed to disappear into the never-ending rear of the plane.

"Nice. I guess if I'm being flown to my eventual death – this is the way I wanna go," Harper said as he leaned back in his chair and rubbed his hands across the soft leather.

"Yeah, it's okay," Kin replied as he started to rifle through his bag of clothes. "I've seen better."

Harper leaned forward in his seat and gave his partner a sour look. "And, *when*, exactly was it that you saw better?"

"Shoot, dude, I don't know. We travel in these things all the time. One just seems to run right into the other. Why are you making such a big deal about it now?"

"I'm sorry," Harper said. "You say 'we' like the two of us get flown around in government jets all the time. I know we're friends and everything, but I do believe this is the first time we've actually flown together anywhere."

"No, not together, but—" Kinley stopped short. "Oh crap."

"Are you kidding me?"

"Harper, don't go get—"

"You are a real piece of work, Kin. Ya know that?"

"Look, bud—"

Harper ran his hands through his hair. "Judas Priest, not only does Kelly give you the best assignments, but she flies you there in private jets like this one?"

Before Kinley could answer, a shapely stewardess walked up to the two gentlemen.

"Good morning, gentleman, my name is Taralyn Tharp. The captain wanted me to tell you that this flight will take approximately one hour and ten minutes. We'll be flying at an altitude of twenty-five thousand feet. In case of an emergency, there are enough parachutes for everyone on board. May I get either of you anything?"

Harper looked up at the attractive flight attendant. "What'd ya have in mind?" he asked without a moment's hesitation.

"Geez," Kinley said under his breath, lowering his head in slight embarrassment. But to his surprise, the flight attendant seemed to warm right up to Harper.

"It's a full service flight, sir," she said.

"Are you a full service – flight attendant?"

"I sure am, sugar," she said.

Harper looked at his friend and winked, "She sure is."

Kinley raised his hand and said, "I'll take a tomato juice and lime. Also a glass of water, a pillow, and a blanket, if that's not too much to ask."

"Not too much at all, sir," the stewardess answered as she walked toward the back of the plane.

"A pillow and a blanket? You going to take a nap, buddy?"

"May as well. You're going to be nailing that stew in about 10 minutes – and don't pretend that you're not."

"And, pray tell, my good man, what is it that makes you think that little hottie is into me like that?"

"Because she didn't take *your* drink order."

The flight attendant returned with her drink cart. She set Kinley's tomato juice and water glass on a table that separated him and Harper, then reached down to the second shelf of the cart to retrieve Kinley's pillow and blanket. She tucked the pillow in snuggly behind his head and spread the blanket out over his lap.

"And for you?" her voice had an almost helpless sound to it.

"Well," Harper leaned over in his chair to look down the middle aisle toward the back of the plane. "I'd really like to know what's back there. Can you show me?"

The flight attendant looked up and down the aisle, then back at the assassin. "Well, maybe you could help me take my drink cart back."

"Oh, I can do that," Harper said standing to his feet. He moved toward the stewardess. "You look really good in that uniform."

As Harper and the woman made their way toward the back of the plane, Kinley pulled his blanket up and tucked it in under his chin. "Holy cow," he said under his breath, "when did I become an extra in a porn movie?"

LAURIE CHASE

Laurie Chase sat quietly on her bed watching the clock on the wall. Three days ago she was part of a DEA covert ops team that had been put in place in Mexico City to fight the drug cartels. It was Laurie and twelve others. She was the communications operative. Doing some good. Making a difference.

But that was three days ago.

Two days ago the team was on an operation to take out one of the biggest drug lords in

South America. His name was Tito del Fuento out of Brazil. He and his team were in

Mexico City for one of the largest cocaine buys in the history of cocaine buys. Laurie Chase had tracked it for weeks and had given her team the best intel possible for the takedown. They were ready to move in and make the bust. But something went wrong.

Not so much something went wrong, so much as everything went wrong. There were no drugs. No blow. No smack. No nothing.

The whole thing was an ambush from the word "go".

Chase was still unsure how she missed it. Was it an inside job from one of her own? Even if it was one of her own, they got what they deserved.

Dead. All of them – the entire team – wiped out in less than ten minutes.

Laurie had been in a van outside the warehouse. The warehouse where everything was targeted to play out. She was the team's eyes on the outside to make sure no one was sneaking up behind them. But it wasn't what was behind them that was the issue.

It was what was waiting for them inside the warehouse.

She played the whole dreadful scene over again in her mind.

"Alpha Team in position, sir," David Bradley's voice crackled across the com.

"Roger that, Alpha Team," came the reply of Kevin Brammer, the ops team commander. "Angel Team, give me a sit ref."

"Angel Team, ready and in position, Commander." Alpha Team was the lead team – the one that would be busting down the front door and getting the fireworks started. Angel Team was coming in from the roof – like angels of death, taking out anything and anyone that was still moving after the first strike from Alpha Team. Sweeper Team, the quartet that Brammer headed, would be the last one to enter from the back of the warehouse. Their job was to clean up whatever was left over from the first two teams.

"Sweeper Team, ready to go," Brammer replied to both of them. "How's it looking out there, Laurie?"

"Clear, sir. Not even a mouse."

"All right. Deep breath, gentlemen. And – Alpha Team on my count – 3…2…1…"

As soon as the team went in – bullets to the brain. The screams that Laurie heard over her com would haunt her for the rest of her life. Alpha Team was down and done in less than a minute. Angel Team was sure they could save the day with an attack from above, but tripwires set to a massive amount of C-4 that was strewn throughout the rafters of the building made Angel Team into a team of angels in seconds.

By this time, Brammer realized what kind of ambush his team had walked into. Watching the top of the building blow off, he knew it was time for a retreat. "Fall back!" he commanded his men as they began to bob and weave through the falling debris. Sweeper Team never even saw the group of men that had flanked them from the rooftop of the neighboring building.

By the time it was over, it was bad guys:12, good guys: 1, maybe.

"Alpha Team!" Can you read me?" Chase screamed into her com as she scrambled toward the front of the van. "Can *anyone* read me? Over!"

Chase climbed into the driver's seat and fumbled with the keys hanging in the ignition. "I repeat: Can anyone hear me? Over?" her voice cracking from the sadness welling up inside her. She turned the key and started the engine, asking once more before driving away, "Please, please, please. Can anyone hear me? Alpha Team? Angel Team? Commander?" Nothing. Just the deafening crackle of dead coms.

Her heart told her to stick around for awhile, just in case. *Somebody had to make it out of there alive, right?*

Her head told her to drive – drive like crazy out of death's way. So, drive away she did. Laurie did not even remember the drive back to the DEA flophouse where she and her team had been set up for the last four months.

All the hours and days and weeks of planning for this operation – wiped out in the short span of about 300 seconds.

Now, a day and a half later, Laurie Chase had been contacted by a general in D.C. who told her about the impending arrival of two government wetwork guys that were going to be there on a top priority mission. She was given a tracking code and told to follow it wherever it went.

No rhyme or reason for any of it, just do it in the name of God and country.

Chase sat quietly on her bed watching the clock and her computer, thinking about her fallen comrades. Funny how in so little time she went from Wonder Woman to Wander Woman. She did not just feel alone. She *was* alone.

The clock struck destiny. Laurie Chase left the flophouse, got into the van, and started to drive to the private CIA airstrip. Two days ago was two days ago. She had a new mission now.

TOUCHDOWN

Harper walked past his partner on the way back to his seat. He tapped him on the shoulder. "I got her number."

Kinley was sleeping well until the tap on his shoulder. He opened his eyes but did not bother moving his head. "That's good. I'm going back to sleep."

Harper sat down in his seat. "I'm worried."

"Geez, Harp, about what?"

"I'm not sure whether to reach out to my new neighbor and ask him to check on my duck or just hope that what I left in his bowl will be enough."

"I'm sorry, what?" Kinley asked as he pulled the blanket down from his head. "Did you just say that you have a *duck* in your new home?"

"Yes," Harper answered, "and I'm not sure I left enough food for him in his bowl. Ya see, I thought that—"

"A real life, Donald Duck – duck?"

"What? Am I speaking in tongues here? Yes. I have a duck in my new home."

"It, lit'rally, just never ends with you, does it?"

"I have a duck."

"Does your duck have a name, perchance?"

"Of course," answered Rowe as if Kinley had just asked him if the sky was blue.

"I can't wait to hear this."

"It's Fudd."

"Fudd? Fudd the Duck?"

"No, not Fudd the Duck. Just Fudd Duck."

"Fudd Duck?"

"Yes."

"That's the name of your pet? Fudd Duck?" asked Devereaux.

"Yes. First name: Fudd – no middle name of The – Last name: Duck."

Kinley pulled the covers back up over his head and mumbled, "Just let me sleep for a few more minutes."

"That's cool," Harper agreed. "The stewardess told me that we have about 23 minutes till touchdown."

"You should get a quick nap, too. We're gonna be up for awhile once we get there." Kinley was quiet for a moment, feigning sleep. "Oh, but wait, you didn't ask for a blanket and a pillow from our airplane Santa, did you?" He opened his eyes for a second, just enough to see that Harper was already out like a light.

"Fudd Duck, we are so screwed."

Laurie Chase had been contacted only a few short hours before the impending arrival of Kinley Devereaux and Harper Rowe to Mexico City, less than 48 hours after the team of undercover agents with whom she had worked had been taken out. It had been a little over a year since they had been inserted into Mexico City.

It was just the thirteen of them, but within the span of 365 days they had done a lot of good. Working together, the group had caused major damage to the South American drug cartels with very little blowback.

Chase was proud of herself and her team for all their work. For the first time in her life, she felt like she was part of something that was bigger than her own meager existence, and part of something that was making a real difference in the world. They had destroyed drug warehouses, brought down drug lords, intercepted major shipments, and had rid the world of some pretty bad guys.

Chase would never forget the live video conference that her team had had with the President of the United States. The President, himself, had commended the team for all the good work that they had done. The President had told them to "hang in there" for another two weeks and replacements would be showing up. All they had to do was complete one last important assignment.

Tito del Fuento. Out of Brazil. Rio, to be precise.

Chase had gone through many channels to find out exactly who it was she was picking up this morning. Still unsure of why her team had been put down like they were, she was afraid to go outside of her usual connections. Nevertheless, she still had some pretty reliable friends in the intelligence business that could dig deep and dig fast to get her the information about which she was inquiring.

Her friends could come up with nothing.

Most of them had their computers frozen and blocked up just for making the inquiry. They let Laurie know that whomever she was picking up, they were some seriously protected government agents.

It frightened her a bit to know that there was no intel whatsoever on the two agents. On the other hand, it comforted her to know that she was going to be working with professionals that knew how to handle their business.

Chase drove quickly through the misty morning. She took mostly main roads, roads that were pretty well trafficked, which is probably why she did not notice the two black jeeps following her to the airfield.

It had been a long day for Harper Rowe and Kinley Devereaux, so it was no surprise when the flight attendant found them both sleeping the sleep of angels. She knelt down beside the duo and said softly, "Wakey, wakey, boys."

Devereaux grabbed his pillow and covered his head with it. "No, Mom, I don't wanna go to school," came his muffled voice.

Harper lifted his head up for a second and tried to blink the fog out of his eyes. He looked over at the stewardess and smiled a sleepy smile. "I'm up."

"Are you?" she asked as she reached over and ran her hand up the inside of Harper's thigh.

"Let me rephrase that; I'm awake." Despite the rephrasing, the assassin did not put up much resistance to Taralyn's advances.

Suddenly, a pillow nailed him upside his head. "Knock it off, ya dopey jerk. I haven't had breakfast yet."

"Sorry, Kin. I was just letting the lady shake hands with Mr. President one last time. Because you just never know whether or not there's going to be a second term."

Devereaux sat up straighter in his seat. "Maybe you'd like to take the flight attendant's make-up case, go in the bathroom, and put your game face on."

The flight attendant stood to her feet. "Fine. I needed to show you two something anyway. Whenever you're ready, if you will just follow me, please."

The two men stared at each other across the table. "Ya'll ready for this?" Kinley grabbed his bag from under his seat and began going through it. "Rats, doesn't look like they bothered to pack my toothbrush." He turned to the flight attendant who was now standing toward the back of the plane, patiently waiting for them. "Got any extra toothbrushes on this plane?"

"Yes, sir, you'll find a full complement of toiletries in the bathroom just past me to the right."

"Sweet." Devereaux grabbed his bag, stood to his feet and said to his partner, "After you, my good man."

Harper walked somewhat wearily up the aisle toward Taralyn. "What is it that you wanted to show us? Can we freshen up first? Is our ride here yet?"

"Well, the captain has given me instructions to make sure the two of you leave here readily armed for – anything."

Suddenly, Kinley and Harper perked up a bit. "Readily armed?"

"For anything?"

"Apparently," Harper said as he looked back at Devereaux, "toiletries are not the only thing they have a full complement of."

"Like I said, gentlemen," Taralyn winked at both of them, "this is a full service flight. So, if you'd like to freshen up first—"

"No, let's see what kind of arsenal we're talkin' about here. My teeth'll wait."

No sooner had he finished speaking than Taralyn opened a door on the right side of the short corridor.

"When you're ready, the bathroom is right in here." She began moving toward the back of the plane. Harper, however, took a slow right hand turn into the huge bathroom.

"Dude, where're you going?"

"I'm gonna freshen up a bit. I'll catch up with you in a few."

"I swear, Harper, if I—"

"Kinley," Harper said in a harsh whisper, "Go, will ya? I'll be up with you in a minute."

PREPARATION

Kinley Devereaux followed the stewardess toward the back of the plane. He towered over her by nearly a foot as they walked down the long corridor. When they reached the end, Taralyn stopped at a door, opened it, and flipped a light switch that illuminated a huge room.

The light blinded Deveraux for a second, but as his eyes adjusted, the room revealed itself. Guns. Weapons of every type. Guns. Knives. Rope. Stilettos. Explosives. Guns. Coms.

Wiretaps. Tracking devices. Guns.

"Good golly. I've died and—"

Devereaux's sentence was cut short by his best friend walking casually into the weapons room. "Don't shoot," Rowe said.

"Come on in, hon," Taralyn said. He, too, looked around in awe, tripping over his own shoes as he did a 360 trying to take it all in. Falling to the floor, he nearly knocked Taralyn over.

"Geez," Kinley said as reached down and pulled Harper to his feet. "Walk much?"

Harper regained his footing and patted Kinley on the back. "Must be that bump I took on the head back there at base camp when that Marine dumped me on my duff like I was yesterday's garbage. I'm cool. We'll not be discussing this with any future girlfriends of mine, but I'm cool."

"Do you have any *past* girlfriends?"

"Some. Not many."

* * *

General David Higgins shut the door of his car. He had just arrived home from dropping Kinley Devereaux and Harper Rowe off at the airstrip. It had been a long night and an even longer morning, and now the sun was high off to his left. His cell phone rang. "Higgins."

"General Higgins, it's Paul Michaels. I've assembled a chaser team that's on standby and awaiting your orders to handle the situation in Mexico City."

"Thank you, Mr. Secretary. As soon as I am ready for them to be deployed I will let you know." Higgins secured the cell phone between his chin and shoulder as he fumbled through his set of keys, found his house key and unlocked the front door. "Other than you and I, Paul, who else knows about our operation?"

"Just my men and me, General Higgins."

"We'll make sure it stays that way." The general entered his home and tossed his keys on the kitchen table. "And what about our other issue? Is that getting taken care of?"

"As we speak, General, but I just want to make sure that you and I are on the same page. You *did* say 'any measures necessary,' correct?"

"Yessir, I sure did."

"Good. In that case, I'll take it from here, General." And just as the United States Secretary of Defense, Paul Michaels, spoke those words, a bullet found its way into and out of the chest of General David Higgins. "Have a good sleep, General Higgins."

* * *

Kelly Campbell rested peacefully on her feather-stuffed mattress topper. She rolled over and sleepily pulled the down comforter up over her shoulder. It had been a long night, and Campbell was finally getting the rest she needed. After being pulled away from Kinley Devereaux, the man she loved and adored – and his good-for-nothing partner, Harper Rowe – Kelly had been debriefed by her boss, Gerald Lange, about all the things that she had seen and heard, and all the things she needed to forget that she ever saw and heard from tonight's little soap opera.

Kelly slept in heavenly peace as Gerald Lange and his family were categorically assassinated – each and every one of them.

*   *   *

"Guess it's about that time, buddy." Harper and Kinley each carried a large black gym bag full of various and sundry weapons. "Ready to get outta here?"

"Are you kidding?" Kinley asked as he took one last look around the room. "I never want to leave the comfort of this place."

Taralyn put her hand up to her ear, was silent for a moment, then said, "The captain has just opened the hatch and is putting the steps down for the two of you to deplane."

Kinley liked her professionalism. Even though he had not had the same opportunities that were offered to his friend, he still felt like he had been taken care of nicely on the all-too-brief flight. Taralyn stepped discreetly in front of the two friends as she led the men toward the open door of the plane. "Right this way, gentlemen."

Harper stepped in right behind the stewardess, and Kinley was quick to follow. Once in line, he grabbed Harper's shoulder.

"What?" Harper asked.

"Well," Devereaux stammered a bit, "do you want a minute alone with her – you know – to say goodbye?"

Harper looked a bit bewildered. "No. Why? Do you want a minute alone with her?"

"No," Kinley said loudly. "I just thought – well, you and her had – ah, never mind."

Firefight

With all that she did not know about her newest assignment, Laurie Chase was relieved to see the private jet sitting at the end of the tarmac of the isolated airstrip. She pulled through the opening in the perimeter fence and stopped. The deplaning steps of the jet had been deployed, but no one had come down them yet.

Harper was the first to emerge. Stepping onto the top flight of the steps, he dropped his black bag of weapons and drew in a long, deep breath. "Judas Priest, it smells like armpits down here."

Kinley stepped out right behind him. "Looks like our chariot has arrived," he said, pointing down toward Chase's van.

From just inside the plane, Taralyn looked out at the scenery. She was the first to see the two black jeeps approaching, with two more right behind them.

"You two need to go now!"

Bullets immediately began ricocheting off the side of the plane. Devereaux was close enough to step back inside and take cover with the flight attendant. But Rowe was already three steps down the stairs. By now, the first two jeeps were within two hundred yards of the plane and gunmen in both vehicles were firing without prejudice. Going down the rest of the steps was certain to get Harper killed, but retreating into the plane was perilous as well. Hearing bullets whiz by and bounce around him, Harper knew he had only one move left. Looking back inside the plane, he caught Taralyn's glance and winked at her. He briefly locked eyes with his partner. "See ya 'round downtown, Kinley!"

With that, Harper grasped his bag of weapons and backflipped over the railing of the deplaning steps.

At first, Laurie Chase was oblivious to what was going on. As much as she wanted to believe that she was over what had happened two nights ago, she knew she was not. In her daydream state of mind, she was missing obvious realtime clues that her own wellbeing – as well as that of her parcels – was in clear and imminent danger.

It did not take her long to snap out of her funk. Perhaps it was the bullet ricocheting off her sideview mirror. Perhaps it was the bullet bouncing off the back of her bullet-resistant van. Perhaps it was the sight of Harper Rowe falling over the side railing of the deplaning steps. Perhaps–.

Whatever it was that snapped Laurie out of her funk also caused her right foot to instinctively tromp down on the gas pedal and lay a bit of rubber as she recklessly guided the vehicle around to the far side of the airplane.

Harper plummeted fifteen feet to the concrete, using his weapons bag to break his fall. By now the quartet of black jeeps had caught up to each other and formed a two-by-two formation as they drove through the fence opening and onto the airstrip. The front and back passenger side windows were down on each vehicle. Gunmen with automatic weapons fired away at the plane, the van, and the man that had fallen and was now taking cover behind the plane's stairs.

Harper reached into his black bag and grabbed the first weapon he could wrap his fingers around. It was a Glock. And while Harper was not a big fan of using guns, it did not mean that he did not know how to shoot like an ace. He took in a deep breath and checked the weapon to be sure it was loaded.

Rolling from his back to his knees to his feet, he crouched up tight against the left side of the steps and started firing.

Taralyn Tharp was not just a beautiful sexy flight attendant for her country's government, she was also a woman of action. This was not the her first firefight and she was not about to cower in the fetal position and wait for someone to save her beautiful ass. As soon as it was clear, she ran to the weapons room at the rear of the plane. A couple handfuls of grenades later, she was back up front with Kinley Devereaux. By now, the pilot and co-pilot had exited the cabin and joined the gun battle. Four grenades – one for her, one for Kinley, one for the pilot, and one for the co-pilot – she handed them out to the trio.

"Apparently these jackasses never have to re-load," the co-pilot noted. Finally there was a break in the barrage of gunfire. Taralyn quickly gave instruction to the pilot, co-pilot, and Devereaux. "You've got 2, you've got 4, you've got 8, and I've got 10," letting them know, clockwise, where each person was to target their grenade. She looked at the pilot. "Go!"

The pilot fired his grenade. The co-pilot fired his grenade. Devereaux launched a strike with his grenade. Taralyn was the last to throw her grenade.

The sight of incoming grenades caused the gunmen to peel back inside their vehicles. The front two jeeps lurched forward, while the rear two jeeps squealed tires in their panic to get out of harm's way. One went to the left behind the fence, the other went right.

For a moment there was silence in the midst of the chaos. Then the ever-soothing voice of Harper Rowe shouted out, "Buddy, c'mon! Now is the time for all good men—" And the grenades exploded.

Kinley Devereaux grabbed his bags of guns and clothes and headed down the flight of stairs. The grenades exploded far enough away that he did not have to worry about shrapnel, and halfway down the steps he could see the mess that they had made.

The two jeeps that had reversed and used the fence as a shield were clear of the shrapnel. The jeeps that had driven forward had stalled their engines. Despite their hasty attempts at re-ignition, they were out of luck, and milliseconds later – out of life. The pilot and co-pilot's grenades did the most damage as their explosions sent multi-sized pieces of metal into the two black vehicles, ripping fatally through the bodies of their eight occupants.

With two steps to go, Kinley jumped over the left railing and landed – feet first – on the tarmac. About twenty feet from his partner and nearly fifty yards from the van, he stumbled a bit, dropping both of his bags.

Once Kinley was clear of the stairs, the co-pilot hit the button to draw them back into the plane's side, making it whole again. The pilot was already back in the cockpit preparing for take off.

Seeing his partner clear the plane's steps, Harper took a moment to note the wreckage that the exploding grenades had caused. Then he grabbed his bag of guns and hurried to the waiting van. Easily beating Devereaux to the open door, Harp threw his bag in and jumped in after it. He turned in time to pull in Devereaux and all his baggage. Kinley – feet barely inside the van door – turned to the driver and said, "Drive!"

"You golden, Kin?" Harper asked.

"Like a rule."

21

HELLO DESMOND

Tara Madison had finally gotten to a safe place with the stolen materials that she had murdered six men over. She knew that Paul Rubello had already set up a meeting spot with the criminal element needed to get top dollar for the stolen property. The only problem was that she did not know who, and she did not know where. What she did know was that there was one other person with all the information she required.

Tara punched in the digits for his phone number. Two rings before he answered with the customary, "Hello?"

"Hello, Desmond. It's Black Ice, baby."

"Ice? You in Mexico City?"

"Yeppers, I sure am. Are you?"

"Just got off the plane about five minutes ago."

"Oh good, then I've caught you just in time," she smiled. "Let me save you an unnecessary trip to see Paul Rubello. I take it that's where you were headed? To see Paul Rubello at the Hotel Habita?"

Timms paused for a moment before asking, "What's going on, Ice? And how—"

"Rubello's dead, Desmond," she interrupted. "He wanted to screw me over on this deal – in more ways than one – so when I started renegotiating my fee – well, let's just say the arbitration talks didn't go well for him. I had to take him and five of his bodyguards out."

"You – you killed Rubello?" Desmond stammered.

"Yeah, honey bunch, that's what I just said. Try to keep up here, will ya? Now I know that you were looking for a bit of a score on the back end with him. Obviously, that's not going to happen at this juncture. Still, I've known you long enough to know that you're a business man, first and foremost, whether it be with him or with me. Am I right?"

Desmond was still trying to wrap his head around the fact that one of his long-time business associates was dead. However, as in most shady underdealings, things were changing on the fly. "Yes, you're right. What exactly did you have in mind?"

"Remember that jewelry store you had me break into a few years back?"

"Yes, I remember it well."

"Okay, there's a motor lodge right down the street from it. I'm in room 17. How long will it take you to get here?"

"Um, let's see," he thought for a few seconds. "I have my bag with me so I just have to go get a rental car, and once I take care of that, I'll be on my way. Shouldn't be much longer than an hour – hour and a half."

"That'll be fine, and, uh, just so I know it's you, knock once, then twice, then three times. Think you can remember that, champ?"

"If I don't, are you going to kill me, too?"

"No. I just won't answer the door. See ya in a few, Desmond." With that Madison ended the call and collapsed onto the bed. She was starting to feel a little more settled with how her plan was coming together, even if the whole thing was being made up as she went along. With Desmond Timms agreeing to work with her, the pieces were beginning to fall into place.

There was just one thing that she was still unsettled about, and that was the man that had gotten closer to her than anyone had ever gotten in the last 10 years. She did not know him, nor had she ever seen him before. Little did she know that over the next 24 hours she would grow to hate him and his name – Harper Rowe.

NEW ALLY

"Welcome to Mexico City!" Chase yelled as she tromped the gas pedal to the floor and screeched tires throughout a perfectly-performed U-turn. Kinley had not yet gotten his bearings inside the van. He rolled awkwardly into Harper and the duo landed against the side wall.

"No need to keep your heads down," Laurie said as she concentrated on the two burning jeeps in her path. "This van is made out of armor-plated metal and bullet-resistant glass."

Kinley and Harper heard what sounded like pings and dings coming from the outside of the van, the sound of bullets ricocheting off the protected vehicle. Harper patted Kin on the shoulder, "You all right, brother?"

"Well, I didn't get shot, but I'd say I'm still quite south of Nashville as far as being okay."

"You're okay," Harper reassured him. He crawled toward the front of the van and got up on his knees to see out the front window.

He could see that the driver had already deftly driven around the two charred jeeps and was speeding toward the airstrip exit. The remaining two jeeps had converged on the opening in the chain link fence and were successfully blocking their path. This second set of eight assailants had gotten out of their vehicles and taken cover on the far side of the jeeps, firing their automatic weapons excessively at the oncoming van.

"Hey, driver, do you have a name?" Harper asked. Without waiting for an answer, he rattled off more questions. "Where's the rest of your team? Why are these people trying to kill us, and who are they? Are you going to ram right through those guys? Because if you are, I just want you to know right off that I have no problem cleaning the grill later on with the remnants of their dead carcasses. Wow – you're not even flinching when those bullets are hitting the windshield."

Without responding, Laurie jerked the steering wheel to the left. The van veered sharply as it avoided ramming the jeeps but sped headlong into the perimeter fence, ramming through it and into a field of weeds and brush.

"Hang on!" she barked as she maneuvered the vehicle across the rutted terrain. After some 50 yards, she got the van back onto the gravel road and floored it, leaving the remaining armed bandits in her dust.

Harper Rowe patted her on the shoulder and said, "That was fun! Can we do it again?"

Devereaux was right over his partner's shoulder when he asked, "Driver, can you please tell us what the Fudd Duck is going on? Where's the rest of your team? And why are there people trying to kill us already? We just got here!"

Harper looked at Kinley. "Not sure if you were paying attention, but I just asked those questions." Rowe turned back to DEA Agent Laurie Chase, "Yeah, it usually takes people a good half hour to get to know us before they start trying to snuff us out like that."

Chase looked in her sideview mirror and saw that the two black jeeps had already started following in pursuit. "I'm pretty sure the guys in the black jeeps are soldiers of Tito del Fuento, and I'm pretty sure they're trying to kill you because they think you're the DEA agents sent down here to replace my team."

Harper looked down and saw that Laurie Chase had a cell phone clipped onto the side of her pants.

"Replace your team? Well, where are they?"

"They're dead," she said bluntly. "Wiped out in a drug raid gone horribly wrong two nights ago." She looked in the rearview mirror to see the two men giving each other looks that were one part confused and one part pissed off.

"I'll take it that you two are just finding this out now?"

"If they were killed two nights ago, then Higgins surely knew about it four hours ago when he sent us down here," Kinley said disgustedly. "I wonder what else he didn't tell us?"

Harper looked at the phone on Chase's waist again. "Kinley, why don't you hop up here in the front seat. No need for both of us to be floppin' around back here."

"You sure?"

"Yeah. I mean, I got to have some fun with the stewardess on the flight down here. Seems the least I can do is let you ride shotgun on the way to our new home."

"Cool. It's about enima uncomfortable back here anyway." Kinley started to move around Harper, and Harper tried to move forward and up against Chase. Kin squeezed by Harper and into the front passenger seat, and as he did, Harper leaned even further into the driver, putting one hand down between her legs.

"Sorry," he said awkwardly – and with his other hand he stealthily removed her cell phone from her hip.

Kinley plopped down in the passenger seat as Harper reeled back into the rear of the van. Suddenly, loud *pings* started sounding off inside the vehicle again as bullets began bouncing off the bullet-resistant metal.

Kinley took a glance in the passenger side view mirror to see both jeeps closing in on them with men hanging out of the windows firing machine guns.

"Doesn't look like they're going to be satisfied until they finish the job – or until we do." He turned around to see his partner pulling apart a cell phone. Harper looked at him and motioned his head toward the driver, signaling Devereaux to keep the driver occupied.

"How do I get this window down?" Kinley asked Chase.

"You can't," she replied as she kept looking intently at the road in front of her. "Bulletproof glass. They don't roll down."

"How are we supposed to fire back at them?"

"We don't. I'm going to have to find a way to lose them, but that's not going to happen on this road."

While the front-seat conversation continued, Harper Rowe was quietly planting a bug into Chase's cell phone. He popped the back off the device and removed the battery. Reaching into the bag of goods he had packed while he was on the plane, he removed one of the thin round listening devices, placed it properly into the phone and had it reassembled within a few seconds. A quick glance toward the front of the van confirmed that Kinley had the driver sufficiently distracted.

The pinging, popping, and dinging of deflected bullets continued. Harper scooched back toward the front of the van and loudly asked, "Hey, driver, you ever hear the expression 'Whatever doesn't kill you only makes you stronger?'"

"Yes, I think I'm familiar with it."

"With all these bullets bouncin' off the van – I'm starting to feel like Superman!" he laughed obnoxiously.

Laurie looked over at Devereaux and asked incredulously, "Is he for real?"

"All too so, I'm afraid."

"I'm sorry, driver – with all the gunfire and what not, we haven't been properly introduced. I'm Harper Rowe. This fine gentleman in the passenger seat is my friend and colleague, Kinley Devereaux." Harper paused for just a moment to see if the driver was going to introduce herself.

She did. "I'm DEA Agent Laurie Chase."

"Well, DEA Agent Laurie Chase, it is a pleasure to meet you. Now—" Harper reached behind him and pulled his black gym bag forward, "my buddy and I have procured enough artillery between the two of us to supply a small third-world army." He reached into the bag, pulled out a grenade, and tossed it onto the dashboard. "Fire in the hole!"

Chase practically jerked the van off the road she was so surprised by the sudden move. She leaned forward to grab the grenade to keep it from rolling around recklessly on the dashboard. The distraction was just enough to give Harper his chance. With expert sleight of hand, he re-attached Chase's phone to her hip.

She finally clutched the grenade in her hand. "What is wrong with you?"

"What? The pin's still in it." Harper took the grenade out of her hand. "These guys that are after us really seem to have some short tempers. In a minute, they're going to have had some short lives, as well. The windows might not roll down on this thing, but that side door opens, and since God blessed me – and neither one of you – with the extra special gift of being a southpaw *and* a great bowler, I'm going to turn those human beings into human have beens."

"How do you know I'm not lefthanded?" Laurie asked.

"Well, for one, when I tossed this grenade onto the dashboard, you grabbed it with your right hand. Whenever a person is in a panic, they instinctively use their strong hand to fix whatever the problem might be. That grenade had rolled almost all the way over to the left side of the dash. If you were a lefty, you would've shown it. For two, you have your cell phone clipped to the right side of your waist. Lastly, when I bumped into you a few seconds ago, I could feel a shoulder holster under your jacket, but no gun on this side which means it's obviously holstered on your left side, exactly where it should be for a right handed shooter."

"You pay pretty close attention for a guy who comes off as a complete jackass."

Harper disregarded her comment. "This van's kicking up so much dust and rocks, I'm pretty sure they won't even be able to tell that I've opened the door. Plus, they're riding so close together I think I can take 'em out with one grenade."

"Why not play it safe and use two," Kinley instructed. "I want to get out of *this* mess so we can get back to the *other* mess we came down here for."

"Point taken, Mr. Devereaux. After all, I am the one that always says if you want to increase your odds of gettin' that 7-10 split, you're best off rollin' two bowling balls." Harper reached into his black bag for one more grenade. He was familiar with these military-issue grenades as he had used them during his several tours in the Middle East. He knew exactly how much time he had from pin pull to release to detonation.

Harper pulled the pins from the two grenades, hit the release lever on the van's sliding door, and slid the door open.

Dust and debris were being kicked up from the tires of the van as Harper squinted his eyes and leaned out the side of the van. He quickly pulled his head back into the vehicle as another onslaught of bullets began.

"Get ready to floor it, driver," he said to Chase. "And..." Harper stuck his left hand, the hand that held both grenades, out the door and tossed the grenades lightly into the air. "Go!"

The momentum from Laurie flooring the accelerator caused Harper to roll back into the van. As he did, Rowe grabbed the van door and slammed it shut. "Let me know how it goes, kids."

Chase and Devereaux watched in their respective sideview mirrors with great anticipation. Like a scene from a movie, they saw the two jeeps riding along, then suddenly shoot into the air simultaneously as the grenades detonated beneath them.

"Nice," Chase smiled and nodded in approval. "You really seem to know what you're doing. I never thought in a million years you'd be able to pull that off."

"Did I get 'em?"

"Bullseye, Harp. Two for two."

"Fist bump?" Harper asked as he crawled up toward his friend and extended his fist.

"No fist bump," Devereaux shook his head as he looked dismissively at his partner's hand. I don't fist bump."

Harper moved his fist toward Laurie Chase. "Fist bump?"

"Do I look like the fist bump type?"

"Chest bump?"

"Harper, knock it off," Devereaux barked as he turned his attention to the driver. "So, do you mind filling us in as to what just happened back there, Agent Chase? Are there going to be more of those guys showing up? And exactly what happened to your team?"

"Like I said before, I think those guys were working for a drug lord named Tito del Fuento."

"Del Fuento? I thought he was in Brazil."

"He is. About a week ago my team was notified that he was coming to Mexico City on a huge drug buy. We figured it had to be huge if he was coming in to supervise the proceedings himself. The intel seemed solid."

"But the night you show up for the bust the party goes south, and your team gets wiped out?"

"It wasn't even close," Laurie said in a very somber tone. "Good men and women that had been working together for years – I was the newb. I figured if something was going to happen badly, it was going to happen to me. We worked so hard on getting the movements for this bust down right. It was going to be one of the biggest in the history of the U.S. DEA." Laurie started tearing up, and her voice broke slightly as she said, "Now they're all gone."

Kinley was looking out the front window and could see the city coming into view. He felt bad for Chase. Her whole world was upside down, and here she was driving two complete strangers into one of the world's most dangerous cities. On the other hand, he felt a little worried that this woman was seemingly coming unglued right in front of him.

Harper, who had positioned himself in a crouched position between the driver's seat and the passenger's seat, patted Laurie on her back. "You're going to be replaying that fight in your head for a long time. You don't have to do it all right now. Just take it a little bit at a time. And – for what it's worth – you're probably the best woman driver I've ever met."

Agent Chase laughed and then sniffled. A sour look overcame her countenance. She had been so caught up in the moment for the last several minutes that she failed to notice it before. "What stinks so bad?" she asked.

"Uh, that's probably me," Harper spoke up. "I've sorta been wearing this same shirt for the last 16 hours or so. Worked up a bit of a lather back there at the airstrip."

"Why have you been wearing the same clothes for so long? That's crazy." Chase took a better look at Harper. "And what exactly is wrong with your face? Did you lose a James Woods look-alike contest or something?" she asked, referring to all the cuts and scrapes on his face as a result of his scuffle with Tara Madison.

"We've had a bit of a tumultuous night," Devereaux smiled. "Let me ask you this: What exactly did they tell you about us? For that matter, did they tell you anything at all? Because they sure as crap didn't tell us anything about you – or the fact that your team had run afoul of a Brazilian drug cartel."

"Not much. I got a text a few hours ago from someone. It just said to call some number, and that it was a matter of national security."

"Still have the number?"

"Yeah, the text is still on my phone."

"Did you call the number?"

"Well, yes, of course. It's not just *anybody* that has access to my phone, and with everything that had taken place in the last 48 hours – yes, I called the number."

"And? Who answered?"

"A man named General David Higgins. Do you know him?"

"Oh yeah," smiled Harper. "Higgy-baby and we go way back. Let me ask you something, Agent Chase: Is he as nice on the phone as he is in person?"

CROOL AND UNUSUAL

It had not been the best of nights for Katie Holt. She was a member of Unit 3, the two-person team in charge of cutting the power to Doug Hopkins' house just long enough for Black Ice and Jason Kilpatrick to gain access to the upstairs safe, and just long enough to add a little more confusion to an already tumultuous scene.

Holt did not know anyone she had seen in the basement last night. She had no clue what was being taken, nor did she have the foggiest idea who the woman was that had given them the plan for the break-in. Her only connection to the whole ordeal was that she was sleeping with the inside man himself, Desmond Timms.

Of course, Katie did not know him as Desmond Timms. She knew him as Devon Harrison. It was Timms that had gotten her on the job and had convinced Madison to give her the cushy assignment of cutting the power. Katie and another woman, Soarse Huygren, had been charged with getting to the two main breaker boxes and, when ordered to do so, cut the power. After that, they were to wait for the commotion to build to a crescendo, turn the power back on, then make a break for it.

Sure, it was not a complete cakewalk, as there were guards posted by each breaker box, but they were disposed of rather easily.

Huygren took the breaker box that was on the outside of the perimeter wall while Katie Holt made her way inside the yard to the box located on the Hopkins' backyard property. As per the plan, the two women were given the verbal order to cut the power – which they did – and just a few moments later they switched the electricity back on.

Soarse Huygren wasted no time in making her getaway. But Katie Holt waited for Madison and the safecracker to exit the house, as she was going to time her escape with theirs. It was just a few short minutes later that Holt thought she heard gunfire coming from the upstairs room. At first she was concerned, but she breathed a sigh of relief when she saw Madison and Kilpatrick exiting the second-floor window.

The two of them were moving at a pretty good clip as they hit the ground running and made a beeline toward the perimeter wall. Just as Holt was getting ready to make her move to catch up to them, she stopped short as she saw a man leap from the second floor window and land in a crumpled mess on the ground. She watched him roll right up onto his feet and take off over the stucco and brick wall in quick pursuit of Madison and Kilpatrick.

Katie waited for him to pass out of sight before she started to move toward the wall. But after taking just a few steps, she saw yet another man jump from the upstairs window.

"What is going on?" she whispered loudly as she retreated back into the shadows. She watched him scale the wall. Just seconds after he disappeared over it, she heard the unmistakable sound of gunfire – a lot of it. Knowing that that particular route of escape was no longer an option, she took off running to the back of the house, hoping to escape the same way she had entered.

It was too late.

The security lights were on in full blaze and security guards had flooded the area. They immediately drew their weapons on her. "Get down on the ground and put your hands behind your head. Now!"

Katie had barely hit her knees before the armed men were grabbing and cuffing her. And they were none too gentle about it, either.

At first, Holt had been placed in the back of a squad car, but she figured it was just a matter of time before the Feds arrived. And she *knew* she would be going with them. Right on cue, a dark gray van pulled up and two intense-looking men in dark suits exited. They talked to some other guys in suits, then they talked to some uniforms, then they were escorted over to the police car where she was. An officer opened the back door to the cruiser and assisted her out. "Ma'am," he said, "these are federal officers. They have some questions that they're going to want to ask you so I'm going to be turning you over to them at this time."

"I'm not answering anything until I talk to my lawyer," she said defiantly. The federal agents walked her over to the side of their van and opened the sliding door on the passenger side.

"Did you not hear what I said?" she asked. "I'm not going anywhere or answering anything until—" Her sentence was cut short as a black bag was placed over her head. "Hey, what the—" Again her sentence was interrupted, this time by a blow to the small of her back. She could feel herself being lifted up and thrown into the van. Her head smashed hard into the wall opposite the sliding door. A few seconds of pain were directly followed by unconsciousness.

As uncomfortable as it was being knocked out, it was even more agonizing being awakened. Two slaps across the face brought Katie Holt back to awareness. Opening her eyes to the blurry image of a federal agent, she looked around the dimly-lit room to see that it was just the two of them. She went to lift her hands to rub the sting out of her jaw only to realize that both of her hands were cuffed to the steel chair she was seated in.

"Katherine Felicia Holt…29 years, 4 months, 3 weeks, and 2 days old…social security number 421-44-4399…you currently have $2,298.44 in a checking account in the Patterson Federal Credit Union…mother's maiden name is Crandle—"

"Okay," she interrupted, "so you know who I am. Who are you, and where's my lawyer?"

The agent moved to the opposite side of the table from where Holt was sitting. "My name is Agent Jeb Crool." He took a business card out of his suit jacket pocket and slid it across the wooden table in Holt's direction. "They call me in from time to time when a situation gets a bit tenuous, and this situation is certainly just that – if not more. As far as where you are – well, let's just say you are currently in a lawyer-free zone."

"No, no, no, you can't do that," Holt objected nervously, her voice cracking a bit. "I know my rights. I get a phone call, at least."

"Don't worry – may I call you Katherine? Do you have a preference?"

"I don't care," came her mumbled response.

"Good. So, like I was saying, Katherine, when this is all over you can press charges against whomever you feel may have offended your inalienable rights, but I'll be upfront with you," Jeb paused for a moment and leaned over the table to drive his point home, the overhead light reflecting off of his shaved head. "You tell me what I need to know, all the charges are dropped, and you can go home to return to your regularly scheduled life, already in progress."

"I'd love to help you out, but I don't know anything."

"Well, you must know *something*. I mean, you knew enough to be at the Under Secretary's house last night when it was robbed. I checked the guest list, and your name wasn't on it so I'm guessing someone else must've invited you there, right? Care to tell me who that was?"

"Look, a friend of mine told me about the job. He told me where to go, and that I'd be given more instructions there. There was this woman there and a bunch of other people. The woman told us what to do, and we did it. I was just the dumbass that got caught. Really, that's all I know."

Katie Holt knew she had a problem because, while it was true that she did not know anyone else in that basement, or the identity of Tara Madison, or what exactly it was that was being taken from the Under Secretary's house, she did know *something* else. One night during pillow talk, Desmond Timms had revealed to Katie that after the job was finished he would be traveling to Mexico City to help assist in the sale of the stolen contents to the highest bidder.

He gave her the where, the when, and the how.

The things men would do and say when the prospect of a little loving was in the air. He was going to be gone for just a few days, returning on Monday night, but he assured her that when he got back – between her cut and his much larger cut – they would have more than enough money to get out of Jersey and relocate down to the islands. Some place nice and warm.

At the time, Katie was happy that Desmond – Devon – had trusted her enough to share this information with her, but now, being handcuffed to a chair with a pretty scary federal agent breathing down her neck, she really wished she did not know as much as she did.

No matter, though. She wasn't going to talk. Give this guy just enough to make him happy, and then she would be on her way.

"This woman – the one that was giving you the instructions – did she have a name?" Jeb started in.

"No."

"What'd she look like?"

"Dark hair. She had it tucked up under a hat. Kinda skinny and—"

"Skinny, how?" Crool cut her off. "Skinny, athletic? Skinny, meth problem?"

"I don't know. Thin, athletic, I guess."

"Okay. What else? What color was she? Black? White? Indonesian?"

"She had dark skin, but the basement was very dark so I don't know if she was mulatto, tanned, or what. I don't know."

Holt's head was really starting to pound now as she was trying to recall what she could about the woman from the basement. "I don't know."

Agent Crool stood up from the desk and started walking around the room. He took his suit jacket off and tossed it on the floor, then turned and faced his prisoner again.

"Look, Katherine, you keep saying that you don't know this, and you don't know that, and it's really getting us nowhere. Here's the thing: I'm on a bit of a schedule which, in turn, means *you're* on a bit of a schedule. So, let me just break this down for you real quick. I'm going to get any information that you have out of you. It's up to you if it's the easy way or if you want to make it more difficult. You decide to go the difficult route, I promise you that you will regret it, and it also means that all deals are off the table. So, whaddaya say, lady? Just answer my questions, and we can all go home."

"I'm trying," she whined.

"How many people were in the basement?"

"Around 10 or 12, I think."

"I'm gonna need your friend's name. The person that told you about the job. Were they in on it, too?"

"No."

"No, what? No, you're not going to tell me the name, or no, they weren't in on it."

"No, he wasn't in on it – so I shouldn't have to tell you his name. It shouldn't matter if he wasn't involved."

"Yeah," Jeb said slowly, "ya see, *his* name is important because it's information. So, if I can't get what I need out of you then maybe I'll go find *him* and see what *he* knows. I don't care if he was there last night, or if he was at the Magic Kingdom smoking a bowl with

Mickey Mouse and Goofy. He knew enough about that job to get you there, didn't he? Which means he's got information that I need. So, I'm gonna need that dude's name, Katherine."

"Fine," she said as she moved her head around in a counterclockwise motion trying to shake some of the pain out. "His name's Kevin."

"Kevin what?"

"Harris. His name's Kevin Harris."

Agent Crool walked around and sat down on the corner of the table that was adjacent to Holt's right hand. He put his foot onto her chair and kicked it around so that she was looking right at him.

"Katherine, apparently you think this is my first day out of interrogation training school, but I assure you that it isn't. I've been doing this for a very, very long time, and I'll admit, I've met some really good liars in my day. People who would look right at me and swear that the sun is made out of Folgers crystals and have me convinced in less than thirty seconds that they were right. I had a certain amount of respect for those people, but you, Katherine, are by far the absolute worst liar I have ever met. Not this week. Not this year. I mean to tell you that you are the worst liar that I have ever met – ever. You've got more tells than a town crier, girlie."

Jeb stood up and started pacing around the room again.

"In all my days of doing this job for the very, very long time that I have, I've learned one thing to be a universal truth, and that is this: people lie because they've got something to hide. *You* are lying because *you've* got something to hide. You're in a world of hurt here, and I'm giving you a chance to come through this unscathed, and yet you take my good nature and you take my good will and throw it right back in my face. Do you know how that makes me feel, Katherine?"

"I'm not lying," she said again, now beginning to come to tears.

"Please, just let me go. I told you everything I know, and you said you would let me go if I did."

"Here's what I'm going to do – and I promise you I'm *not* lying. I'm going to walk outside that door for a minute, and when I come back you're going to tell me what it is that you're lying about. My time for being nice to you is just about over, but my time for making your life a miserable, gut-wrenching, pain-filled agony – well, that's just about to get started."

He walked over to the table, leaned over it, and looked hard at Katie Holt with his steely gray eyes. "Now, you just think about that, Katherine, and I'll be right back."

As she watched him walk out the door she yelled, "Just let me out of here, you sick psychopath!"

24

HOME BASE

During the long ride back to the flophouse where the DEA agents had been staying in Mexico City, Laurie related the conversation she had had with General David Higgins about Kinley and Harper, and just exactly what it was that he wanted the three of them to accomplish with regard to Tara Madison and the stolen contents which were in her possession.

Upon arriving in the city, the trio went through tedious measures to make sure that no one was on their trail. As they drove Chase informed the two men about certain areas of the city – parts that were nice, parts that were extremely dangerous, and areas where she had seen people kidnapped right off the street in broad daylight. Mexico City, while it had its fair share of tourist attractions, was a very bad city for caucasians to walk around in, either by themselves or in a small group. They were often kidnapped by drug cartels and were either held for ransom or just slain for reasons known only to the kidnappers.

The trio parked the van in an underground lot and walked about three blocks over back streets and alleys until they came to a beat-up doorway that led into an even more beat-up building.

Harper and Kinley were tired.

Carrying their respective bags over their shoulders, the three-block walk left them breathless with sore and burning leg muscles.

"I see our government spared no expense on this one," Harper said quietly, as they entered the building. A dimly lit hallway led to a dingy stairwell and the three flights of stairs that led to a third floor apartment.

"This is it," Chase said as she unlocked the door knob and a deadbolt and led Devereaux and Rowe into the less-than-deluxe accommodations. "You can drop your things here for now."

As if unburdening themselves of anvils, the two dropped their bags to the floor and rotated their shoulders and stretched their backs.

"Where can I find the bathroom?" Harper asked. "I've got a Nagasaki-sized bomb that needs dropping and now."

"You *are* nothing but class, aren't you?" Chase quipped. "The bathroom's down that hall and to your left. It's the one with the toilet."

Casting a quick glance at Devereaux, Harper gave an indistinct nod toward his partner's ear – a silent allusion that he would soon be communicating with Kinley through his com – and then began a quick walk toward the bathroom.

"Come on in, Mr. Devereaux," Chase instructed. "I'll give you a tour of the place." Kinley followed her into a shabbily furnished living area. "This is the living room – couch, rocker, recliner, tv – and in there," she pointed to her right, "is our almost fully-functioning, but rarely used kitchen." Kin followed her through the living room and into a much larger room that was wall-to-wall electronics. "And in here is our communications room."

For being such a hole-in-the-wall apartment, Devereaux was impressed with the setup of computers, phones, surveillance equipment, and various other electronic equipment that crowded the area. But he guessed that was the idea – who would ever think of looking for a multi-million dollar communications center in a hole like this? He watched as the female agent walked over to one of the computers, took a seat in the adjoining chair, and gave a slight nudge to the mouse to bring the monitor to life. "You can make yourself at home wherever you want. I'm going to check for any updates or new information on our situation."

Suddenly, a familiar voice crackled in Kinley's right ear. "Hey, buddy, can you hear me?"

"Yeah," he replied to Harper. To Laurie Chase he said, "I think I'll do that – relax a little. You have another bathroom where I could wash up a bit?"

"Yeah, sure," she said without looking up from her task at hand. "The master bedroom at the end of the hall has a bathroom in it. Let your partner know that there are some clothes in the other bedrooms. Unless he's weirded out by wearing the clothes of dead men, he should be able to find something that fits him."

"Sweet doin's. Tell 'er I said 'thanks,' will ya?" Harper buzzed through the com.

"Thanks. I'll let him know, Laurie. And I didn't really have much of a chance to say anything earlier, but for as lousy as this whole setup is, I'm looking forward to working with you. Get this mess figured out."

He stood there in silence waiting for some sort of reply from Chase. But after a few moments without even a nod of her head to acknowledge what he had just said, Devereaux shrugged his shoulders, turned on his heels, and headed toward the hallway in search of his partner.

Harper Rowe had found a first aid kit in the bathroom. After removing some cotton balls from it, he looked in the medicine cabinet behind the bathroom mirror to find a bottle of rubbing alcohol. He put a cotton ball over the mouth of the bottle then took the alcohol-soaked puff and began to dab it onto all the little wounds left by the gravel that was propelled into his face by Tara Madison's getaway, literally making him eat her dust. As he felt the sting of the alcohol sterilizing each wound, Kinley appeared at the bathroom door.

"You need any help with that, bud?"

"No, I think I got it," Harper replied through clenched teeth. "Judas Priest, this stings like a mother, though."

"Hey, good job, by the way," Kinley said in a hushed tone, "getting that bug into her phone. Smart move on your part."

"Well, good job on your part, too," Rowe said in an equally hushed tone, "keeping her distracted long enough for me to do my job."

"I don't think I kept her distracted as much as the drug-crazed idiots that were shooting at us."

Harper gently touched the cotton ball to the last of the cuts on his face and for no apparent reason said, "We're probably going to die down here."

"I'd just as soon we didn't,"Devereaux said.

"Think we're golden?" Harper asked.

"Like a pond, baby. Like a golden pond."

"I had to get that bug in there, though, because I'm telling you right now, Kin – the way this thing's playing out, I don't trust anybody that ain't you and me."

Harper threw the scarlet-tinged cotton ball into the trash can. He grabbed a nearby towel, looked in the mirror, and gingerly pressed the towel to his face to soak up the remaining blood and rubbing alcohol.

"Yeah, you're not kidding. This whole thing stinks of lies and corruption. I just don't know *whose* lies and *whose* corruption. I still don't even know why in God's name they sent *us* down here. Because we saw her up close, and nobody else ever has? That doesn't even make any sense."

"And they conveniently forget to tell us that the team of DEA agents we're supposed to work with doesn't even exist anymore. I mean, for as screwy as this whole situation is, I was pretty cool with it up until that point."

"Plus, now that we're here," Kinley shook his head back in forth in bewilderment, "I don't even know what we're supposed to do."

"Well, first things first. Let's go see if we can't find me some clothes."

CONFESSION

Jeb Crool walked back into the interrogation room, and this time he was not empty handed. This time he was carrying a silver metal case, and he walked directly to the table where Katie Holt was sitting and set it down flat. He popped open the two fastening levers on the front panel.

"And you're sure you don't have anything else to say?"

By now Holt had stopped crying and returned to the stone-faced demeanor that she had had when the questioning first began. "No," was her simple and definite answer.

"That's pretty much what I thought." Crool lifted the lid of the case to reveal a large hypodermic needle and several vials of liquid, all of which were encased by dark gray styrofoam.

Holt, who had not removed her icy gaze from the interrogation room floor since Agent Crool had walked back in, now did. Looking apprehensively at the contents of the case, she tried to control her fear. But her voice trembled when she asked, "What is that?"

"It's called hyoscine pentothal. Ever heard of it?"

"No," she answered nervously.

"Well, that's because technically"—Crool made air quotes with his fingers— "it doesn't exist."

"What does that mean, 'it doesn't exist'?"

"It means that if the FDA or the AMA or even one of those government human rights agencies thought for a second we used this drug the way we do – they'd probably be putting us into jail without so much as a single charge being filed, much less any sort of a trial being held. But, fortunately, for me, and unfortunately for you, no one knows of its existence – much less the fact that I'm using it as a form of interrogation enhancement."

"Is it going to kill me?"

Crool gave an incredulous laugh. "Oh, Katherine, you really are a special kind of stupid, aren't you? I'm trying to get information out of you. What on earth makes you think that I'm going to be able to do that with you being dead?"

Before she had time to answer, the interrogator continued. "No, no, my dear, this chemical concoction won't kill you. It will just make you wish that you were dead. Imagine that every nerve ending in your body is on fire – on fire and burning through your skin. Can you do that for me? Can you imagine pain like that?"

Her throat suddenly felt tight and it was hard for her to swallow. She felt all the color leave her face and a nauseated feeling welled up in her stomach.

"Ya see, Katherine, now is the time when you really need to think long and hard about how much you want to protect this *Kevin Harris*," again with the finger quotes, "or whomever it is that you're lying for. Things are about to get extremely dicey for you."

The nauseated feeling broke inside her stomach, and she wretched up a good amount of bile and saliva which was followed by uncontrollable coughing and dry heaving.

"That's it, kid. Get it all out of your system." Crool walked around the table and stood behind Holt. While she was doubled up in pain and still spewing remnants of her stomach contents onto the floor, Jeb reached down and pulled her hair back away from her face. With a comforting voice he said, "You're going to be all right. Just take it easy, kid. You're going to tell me what I need to know, and we're gonna get ya outta here and into a nice bed where you can sleep for awhile."

After a few more seconds of vile human sounds and some crying and coughing, Katie finally sat back up straight in the chair. She had tears running from her eyes, mucus coming out of her nose, and saliva and spittle dripping down her chin. Agent Crool took a handkerchief from his pants pocket. He then reached into the opposite pants pocket and retrieved the handcuff key and used it to unlock her right wrist. He handed her the handkerchief, "Take a minute and clean yourself up. Get yourself together and let's talk about what you really know."

Holt took the handkerchief from the agent and wiped off her chin and blew her nose a few times before she finally wiped away the tears that were rolling down her cheeks.

"You ready to talk now, Katherine? Because I really don't want to have to put this stuff into you, and judging from your reaction there, I'm pretty sure you don't want me to have to put this stuff into you, either."

Katie finished drying her tears. She looked at Agent Jeb Crool and nodded. "I'll tell you what I know."

Twenty minutes after Katie Holt's full confession, the phone in Secretary of Defense Paul Michaels's study rang. It rang only once as he was quick to answer.

"Tell me something good," he barked into the receiver.

"We got it, Paul. Jeb Crool was able to extract the information for us."

"Crool. He does have a way with people, doesn't he?"

"That he does, Mr. Secretary."

"Well, give it to me, son. We don't have a lot of time here."

*   *   *

Kinley and Harper had found their way into a back bedroom inside the apartment. Kin had taken a seat at the foot of the bed while his shirtless buddy rifled through a bureau drawer to find something that looked like it would fit comfortably. One by one, Harp pulled each shirt out and held it up in front of his face, analyzed it, then sloppily folded it up and put it back into the drawer.

"So, the bug you put in her phone," Devereaux said quietly, "it's linked into our coms, right?"

"Absolutely. We'll be able to hear any incoming and outgoing calls that she receives and makes." Harper finally found a dark gray three-button long-sleeve henley shirt. He pulled it over his head, put his arms through the sleeves, and slid it down around his athletic torso. "This look all right?"

"Yeah, man, it looks fine."

"I know we've got to stay focused on the task at hand, but – we need to seriously consider the possibility that we might not get out of this unscathed. With all the lies that we've been told up to this point, I'm seriously beginning to think that we might be disposable commodities in the big picture here. I keep thinking about what Steve Robbins said back at the Pentagon about us being as disposable as yesterday's trash. If it comes down to it, do you have a back door out of this situation, Kin?

"I don't know. I'd really rather not think about that at this point." Devereaux laid back on the bed and ran his hands through his thin-shaved dark hair.

"Hey, I don't want to think about it either, but if it *should* get to that point, I've got some paperwork in a safe deposit box in a bank about 20 minutes from here. New identities, new passports, driver's license, birth certificate – the whole nine."

"Yeah, okay, I appreci—"

Devereaux's sentence was cut short as he and Harper simultaneously heard Laurie Chase's cell phone ring through both of their coms. The two men exchanged a quick look. Devereaux bolted upright on the bed.

"Here we go," Rowe said.

Both of them staring straight ahead, listening intently. Both of them wondering who was going to be on the other end of this call.

Chase answered her phone, "Agent Laurie Chase."

TIMMS AND MADISON

Desmond Timms walked casually up to the door of room 17, taking in his surroundings to make sure there was no one lurking in the motel parking lot waiting to jump him. Satisfied that he was alone, Timms performed the prearranged knock. A few seconds later the door swung open just a bit and Madison waved him in. After he had entered she, too, stuck her head out the door to make sure that no one was around.

"You're late," she said.

"Yeah, sorry about that, but I thought I had picked up a tail at the airport so I took the long way here. I either lost him, or I was just being paranoid. One can never be too safe these days. Speaking of which, I was hearing about your handiwork on the radio during my ride over here. What exactly brought on the sudden change of heart? And why should I trust you not to plug me, too?"

"Rubello was a jackass – a pompous and arrogant one, at that."

"I know a lot of jackasses. I never thought enough of them to want to kill them, though, but I guess we all have our own ways of dealing with things."

"Do you know what I stole last night, Desmond?"

"Yeah, I know exactly what you stole: a thumb drive with some blueprints on it."

"Not just any blueprints," Madison shut the door, locked the knob lock and the deadbolt, and reconnected the safety chain. "Blueprints to something that will change the world as we know it. And you know how much he was going to pay me for these?"

"I have no idea, Ice."

"A hundred large." Madison walked to the mini-fridge across the room. "Beer?"

"No, thanks," he declined. "A hundred large, huh? So, what do you think would've been a good fee? What would Paul have to've given you in order for you not to kill him – and the other five guys? Nice work by the way."

"A little honesty would've been nice. Those blueprints on that thumb drive are going to pull hundreds of millions of dollars – maybe even into the billions – and he thought paying me one percent when I did all the hard work was going to fly? Not to mention, I'm pretty sure he was going to try to have his way with me, physically." Tara grabbed a bottle of beer from the small refrigerator, shut the door, and turned back to face Timms.

"Hold up. Did you just say 'billions'? With a 'b'?"

"I did, yes."

"Son of a bitch. Rubello was only gonna give me 300K for my part, and I was at the house *and* set up the meeting with the buyers. I'm glad you shot his ass now."

"Well, that's why I'm willing to split whatever we get 50/50, right down the middle, okay? I need you to get me to the meet with the buyers, and you need me to deliver the package." Madison popped the top off of the *botella de cerveza*. "So, what do you say, Desmond? Partners?"

Timms smiled wryly and asked, "Now how do I know you're not just gonna shoot *me* when the time comes, Ice? And how, exactly, did you know that I was the one setting up the meet?"

"Last words of a dying man," she said without expression.

Desmond hesitated for just a moment before he finally nodded and said, "Yeah. All right. Partners it is then, but from here on out – you and me are connected at the hip. Where you go, I go, and vice versa. We straight?"

"I got no problem with that, Dez. I do my part, you do yours, and we both leave this town richer than our wildest dreams. I don't know about you, *partner*, but I'm going someplace warm with no extradition laws."

"I couldn't've said it better myself, but let's not get ahead of ourselves. I told Rubello that there wouldn't be any time to sit on this drive. It's not going to be long before the feds or whoever it is catches up with us. The meet is going down tonight, Ice. 10 p.m. on the roof of the east tower of the Twin Towers Polanco."

"The roof? Kind of an open space, don't you think?"

"There's going to be representatives there from over 20 – maybe 30 – different countries. I needed a space that was going to be accommodating enough for the crowd. Plus, I've got my own security detail setup that's going to make it impossible for anyone to make a break for it should they get the bright idea of trying to pull some kind of tomfoolery or hijinx."

"What's your security layout going to look like? The Polanco Twin Towers is a pretty big skyscraper."

"I'll have guys in the stairwell to check all guests for weapons before they can even come up on the roof. I'll have heavily armed guys all around the perimeter of the roof, guys on the roofs of surrounding buildings to make sure no one has any thoughts of firing off a few rounds to cause some sort of disruption or distraction in an attempt to make off with the package. I'll also have guys down on the ground surrounding the building so that once things get underway at 10 p.m. – no more admittance. Plus, they'll be keeping an eye out on the ground to make sure that no cops, feds, or any Johnny Law types show up without giving us a good head start to get outta there in one piece."

"Have you told anyone else about this? We don't need any loose wires out there giving away our position."

For a moment he thought about Katie Holt. He was concerned that he had not heard from her yet. But then, right on cue, Timms's phone rang and Katie's cell number flashed on the screen. He held up his index finger to Tara, "Hold on one sec, Ice. I gotta take this."

Desmond put his phone up to his ear. "Hello."

"Devon? Are you alright? Are you in Mexico City?"

"Yeah, I'm fine. How about you?" Devon began to make his way toward the door, but Madison pulled her Blackhawk pistol and casually put the nose of it into Devon's stomach.

"Put that on speaker phone," she whispered in his ear.

He put his hand over the phone. "It's a personal call, Ice."

"*Connected at the hip*, isn't that what you said? Put it on speaker phone, or I walk out of here right now – after I shoot you."

"Fine." Desmond pressed a button on his phone, and said to Katie, "Katie Holt, you are now on speakerphone with myself and – a friend of mine."

"That's fine. I just wanted to call to let you know that I made it home safely. Are you still planning on being back here tomorrow night?"

"I am," he smiled at Black Ice and shook his head *no*. "Well, thanks for calling, Katie. Glad you made it back okay. You didn't have any problems did you? I kinda thought I might hear from you sooner than now."

"I just wanted to make sure you had landed before I called, is all. I knew you wouldn't have your phone powered up on the plane so I just waited until I was sure you were on the ground. Everything is fine."

"Good. Okay, then I will plan to see you at the airport tomorrow night when you come to pick me up."

"I'll be there, Devon. See you then."

Desmond ended the call and looked at his new partner. "So, were you really going to shoot me if I had kept walking out the door?"

"It doesn't really matter if I would have or wouldn't have. What matters is that you *believed* I would have." Tara smiled. "Let's make a deal, partner. For the next 24 hours, you and I are of one mind and purpose: getting the most money we can from this deal. I've got the package, and I know that I could get a lot of money for it, but that would entail me doing a *lot* of legwork. Globetrotting the world to find my highest bidder isn't something that I'm *not* willing to do, but when I know you've already done the legwork, and you've already got the world globetrotting here to do the bidding themselves – well, it just seems a sin to waste all the time and effort that you already have invested into this deal, Desmond." Madison ran her finger across the lips of Timms's mouth. "So, do try to stay focused, okay, sweetie?"

On the other end of that conversation, Katie Holt hung up the phone and looked at Jeb Crool. They were still in the interrogation room. "Satisfied?" she said coldly.

"Yeah. Yeah, I think I am." Agent Crool turned to a security guard that was standing just inside the door. "You can go ahead and take her."

"What's going to happen now?" Holt asked as she was helped to her feet from the chair by the guard. "You said if I cooperated things would go easier for me."

"Yeah, well, that was before you told me 17 lies in a row, Katherine. Alex here is going to take you to a holding cell so you can get some sleep while we figure out what to do with you. If we can nab your friend and his accomplices and get our property back, things will go all right for you."

"What if you don't? What then?"

"Then I'm afraid things *aren't* going to go all right for you."

The guard led Katie Holt out of the room and out of sight. Jeb Crool's partner, Agent David Baldwin, came into the room. "Nice work, Crool. Did you use the ol' hyoscine pentothal routine on her?"

"Absolutely. She went for it hook, line, and sinker, too."

"You're a jackass."

"Yeah, but I'm an effective jackass, Dave. I had her call the guy that got her in on this gig. She says his name is Kevin Harris – or maybe it was Devon Harris. Whatever it is, he confirmed that he *is* in Mexico City, and he's there with somebody else, too. Could be Black Ice – could be anyone though."

"So, who's going down there to get this Kevin Harris guy then?"

"From what I understand, there's already a team in place down there. They were dispatched early early this morning. I hope whoever it is can get this job done, and quick. I don't know what was stolen, but it's got some major heads calling in favors from all over the place. Our next step is to find out who Kevin or Devon Harris really is. Apparently, he is the one that is setting up a meeting tonight to sell whatever it was that was stolen."

"I just don't understand it, Jeb. If this was some kind of sting operation to lure this Black Ice character out into the open, why the heck was there something legitimate for him to steal?"

"Because, Dave, *she's* just that good. There have been so many other attempts to force her out into the open without having any meat on the hook, and somehow she always sniffed it out. This time they put something out there that they knew would entice her, but whatever it was, she wasn't supposed to get away with it. Now that she has, the clowns can't get out of the car fast enough."

"You keep saying *she*. I thought Black Ice was a man."

"That's just how good *she* is. Till now Black Ice has managed to be so elusive and clever that no one had ever seen her. Not on security cameras, no eyewitnesses, not even as much as a reflection on a plate glass window."

Baldwin just shook his head in bewilderment. "I sure hope whoever it is that they sent after her can get the job done. Sounds like the sooner we can get this mess cleaned up, the better off we're all gonna be."

The Mystery Man Revealed

With Laurie Chase's cell phone conversation loud and clear in their coms, Kinley Devereaux and Harper Rowe waited with intense anticipation to hear who the second participant in the colloquy was going to be.

"Agent Chase," they heard a man's voice say, "is this a secure line we're on?"

"Absolutely. This is my cell phone, and it hasn't left my possession since I have been here."

Kin and Harper exchanged a quick glance. Harp gave an evanescent smirk and they resumed their intent listening.

"May I ask with whom it is I'm speaking?"

"Agent Chase, this is the United States Secretary of Defense, Paul Michaels. I wanted to call you and speak to you personally about everything that has taken place over the last 15 hours and, more importantly, what will be taking place in the hours to come."

In the back bedroom, Kinley and Harper again exchanged quick looks at one another, only this time there were no smirks or smiles of any kind. Instead, the two men shared equally puzzled expressions. "Are you kidding me?" Devereaux said quietly. "Paul Michaels? The Secretary of Defense?"

"Mr. Secretary, to what do I owe the honor?" Chase's tone was now cloaked in reverence.

"Agent Chase, please, it is I who am honored. It has been brought to my attention how much heroism and courage you have displayed in the past 72 hours. However, as much as it displeases me to say this, your country needs you now more than ever."

"Sir, I assure you that whatever it is that is required of me, I am more than ready to do it."

"Agent, I can't think of anything that could please me more than to hear you say that – which is precisely why I wanted to call you myself. Agent Chase, once you have completed this assignment, the details of which we will cover momentarily, you can consider your duties to your country completed – paid in full – and the world, as they say, will be your oyster."

"Umm, I don't think I understand, sir."

"Agent Chase, what I'm telling you is that once you've successfully completed the tasks that I'm getting ready to assign you, you can retire. Go where ever it is that you desire, do whatever it is you want to do – with whomever you want to do it – and your country will foot the bill. If you want to move into a penthouse apartment that overlooks the strip in Las Vegas, you can. If you want to move into a quaint little cottage in the Swiss Alps and spend your evenings sipping on hot cocoa while watching musicals with your Alaskan husky, Sundance, you can do that, too. If you want to set yourself up in Aruba and spend your days drinking fruity drinks with those little umbrellas in them – consider it done. Do I need to go on, Agent Chase, or have I drawn a decent enough picture to answer your question?"

"No. No, sir. I – uh, I just – I just don't know what to say," Laurie stammered and stuttered.

"Your undeniable love for your country and your undying patriotism says it all, Agent Chase."

Devereaux, who was now sitting on the edge of the foot of the bed, began feigning the "jacking off" motion with his right hand and quietly said, "Enough already with this butt-kissing contest, gang. Can we please get on with this?"

"Okay, Agent," Paul Michaels continued, "now that I've given you the good, it's time for the bad. I've offered you such a sweet deal because this situation is dire, and – even though I know we would both like for the circumstances to be any kind of different – this is the hand that we've been dealt. Mr. Devereaux and Mr. Rowe are there to assist you, but you are my point man on this operation. Do you understand? I will deal directly with you, and you will deal directly with me. No go betweens on this one. I'd love nothing more than to ask you if you're up for the challenge, Agent Chase, but you are my only option. Still, circumstances being what they are, I have the utmost confidence in your abilities to complete this assignment and get the necessary results that we so desperately need."

"May I ask, sir – what, exactly, are those necessary results?"

"First and foremost, the stolen contents from last night must be recovered immediately. On this point there is absolutely no room for error or compromise. Secondly, it would be optimal – but not necessarily an absolute – for those responsible to be eliminated, for they are not only enemies of this great country, but they are also both real and imminent threats to its well-being. The two men that are there with you, Mr. Devereaux and Mr. Rowe, are highly trained in the art of removing such threats. Again, just to reiterate, the elimination of the target is very much secondary to the recovery of the contents that they currently possess."

"The priorities of the mission seem very clear, Mr. Secretary."

"I've just been given solid intel that the stolen material will be out in the open tonight. This will be the one and only time that you will have to recover and secure it, Agent Chase. I'm ready to give you this information so, please, let me know when you are ready to write it down."

"Wouldn't it be easier just to send me the intel in an email, or, perhaps, text it to my phone?"

"Agent Chase, when I asked you earlier if this was a secure line, it's because I don't want anyone overhearing this conversation. In turn, I sure as hellfire and brimstone do not want to leave a paper trail for someone to come along two weeks from now and go sniffing around on. I cannot stress to you enough that what has happened – and what is going to happen – is a matter of national security. The secrecy and confidentiality of the item that was taken last night are of the utmost importance. I know the current administration is all about transparency, and, while that's a nice notion to get someone elected to a political office, what we are getting ready to discuss is for you and whomever you deem vital in the task of this mission. Are we clear on that detail, Agent?"

"Yes sir, Mr. Secretary. The clearest."

"Also, the deal that we just discussed as far as your future is concerned – that stays between you and me. Mr. Devereaux and Mr. Rowe will be getting their own deals soon enough, and there's no need to be comparing notes on who's getting what after this is over. Understood?"

"I understand, sir," Chase acknowledged.

In the back bedroom, Harper and Kin looked at each other. "Somehow I get the ominously crappy feeling that our deal isn't going to be nearly as good as hers," Harper commented. "That's even if there *is* a deal for us. Something tells me that we shouldn't be holding our collective breaths too long for that one."

"I just can't believe this chuckwagon is cutting us out of the loop like he is. At least, he was nice enough to give us props for being *highly trained, threat removal artists.*"

"Yes, and both kinds of threats, at that – the real *and* the imminent."

Totally oblivious to the prying ears of the two assassins, Paul Michaels and Laurie Chase resumed their conversation. "Should I get Mr. Devereaux and Mr. Rowe for this part of the conversation, sir? Unless there are other things that you and I need to discuss in private?"

"I don't think you understand, Agent Chase, *you* are my point man on this operation. I'm going to give *you* all of the intel that we've collected from our end. What you choose to tell them or not tell them, and any planning procedures from here on out will be totally up to you. This is your show. I will be dealing with you and you alone."

From their peanut gallery at the back of the apartment, Harper and Kinley continued their wisecracks. "Is it my imagination or didn't we already cover this?"

"Yeah, the 'I'm Dealing With You And You Alone' lesson was about two sessions ago. It was right before the 'Mission Directive Priority List' and the 'Don't Tell Your New Partners How Badly I'm Going To Screw Them When This Is All Over' lessons were given."

"Mmmm, mmmm, mmmm," Devereaux shook his head sadly back and forth. "And to think – they want to put *her* in charge."

"Yeah, but I did hear that you and I finished a very respectable fourth place in the in-charge balloting."

"Very funny. Now shut your piehole. I think this is the part where we're supposed to pay attention."

"Here's what we know right now, Agent Chase," Paul Michaels continued, "we know that an international thief that goes by the alias 'Black Ice' stole contents that were vital to the national security of the United States. With the use of some airport security cameras and some recent intel that we were able to uncover last night, we have been able to track Black Ice to Mexico City. Since no real intel as to the identity of Black Ice exists, we've sent you the next best thing."

"The next best thing, sir?"

"Yes, that's right, Agent. You see, Mr. Devereaux and Mr. Rowe are not only highly skilled assassins, but, from what I've been told, they've both been face-to-face with our assailant just as recently as last night. They'll be able to help you identify Black Ice when she brings the contents out into the open."

"And do we have any idea as to where and when that – I'm sorry, did you just say that Black Ice is a *she*?"

"According to the description that was given to us via Mr. Devereaux and Mr. Rowe, yes, Black Ice is, indeed, a woman. Now, to answer the first question that you didn't ask: yes, again. As I was telling you earlier, we do know where and when the stolen property is going to be out in the open. We have been given solid info that the people in possession of said property have a meet set up with potential buyers tonight. It is set to take place on top of the Santa Fe East Tower of the Polanco Twin Towers at 10 p.m. local time in Mexico City. Are you familiar with the Polanco Twin Towers, Agent Chase?"

"Yes, Secretary Michaels. Not only familiar with the location, but also very familiar with the building itself."

"Very good to hear. Now, Agent Chase, I need for you to listen to me very carefully..."

Harper Rowe, who had been leaning up against the tall bureau of dresser drawers from which he had removed the shirt that now adorned his torso, nodded to his partner and said quietly, "I think this is that 'paying attention' part you were alluding to earlier."

"...I don't really care what you do or how you do it – you can use an army of spider monkeys for all I care – but you can *not* let those contents get off that roof. We have tracked them about as far as we can. I am leaving this all in your hands. If that stolen property makes it off that roof, it will be too late to do anything else."

"I understand, sir. Please don't spend a moment fretting about those contents making it off of the top of that roof, Mr. Secretary. We will succeed."

"That's what I like to hear, Chase." Paul Michaels pulled his head away from the phone to clear his throat, and then he re-commenced with his speech. "Once you've come up with some semblance of a plan, I want you to call me, tell me what it is, and let me know what you need from us up here. I just want to let you know that anything you need from us here in Washington D.C. is at your ready, Agent Chase."

"Do we know where the contents are currently, sir?"

Harper winced and looked to Kinley, "Ooohhh, not a good question to ask, sweetheart."

"I think she's fixin' to get yelled at here," Devereaux agreed.

"I'm sorry, Agent Chase. Did you just ask me if we know where the stolen contents are – currently? Because if you did, I would just like to know what, exactly, that means?"

Laurie stuttered and stammered a few moments.

"You know," Kinley said as he reached down to touch his toes and stretch his back, "she would really impress me here if she would reach down, grab herself a set, and ask this useless little prick just what it is, exactly, that's on those stolen contents that's got everybody so up in arms."

"Yeah, and if *if*s were clouds and clouds were elephants, we'd all have our own little safari, now, wouldn't we?"

"Attention Kmart shoppers, we are currently running a blue-light special on all adult khaki shorts in aisle seven. That's a blue-light special on all adult khaki shorts in aisle seven."

Secretary of Defense Paul Michaels started in again.

"Agent Chase, I assure you that if I – or anybody else in this office – knew where those contents were right now…don't you think we would've gotten in touch with you before this?"

"Yessir, Mr. Secretary," Laurie answered bashfully.

"Agent Chase, I am here for you every step of the way. We have the world's greatest intelligence capabilities at hand, so don't you ever think that anything you need is too big for you to ask for or too hard for us to get. Figure out some semblance of attack and get back to me as soon as you do. Once you do that we can start planning the next stages of this operation. Do you have any questions for me right now, Agent Chase?"

"Ask 'im, kid," Devereaux said.

"Yeah, ask him the million dollar question, chica," Harper echoed. "You know you want to know."

Chase bit her lower lip thoughtfully. After totally putting her foot in her mouth with her last question, she was hesitant to ask another, but, still, she wanted to know. "What are we trying to recover, Mr. Secretary? The stolen contents, I mean. We'll need to know what we're looking for so that when we intercept the contents, we'll know that we have the right contents."

"Score!" Kinley and Harper shouted together.

Paul Michaels was silent.

"Mr. Secretary?"

"Get your team and your plan together, Agent. Call me back," and with that the Secretary of Defense was gone.

"Hello?" Laurie pulled her cell phone away from her ear and gave it a confused look. Hello?" she said again.

28

Kelly Campbell Checks In

SATURDAY MORNING
11:39 A.M.

The back bedroom of the U.S. Drug Enforcement Agency flophouse located on the west side of Mexico City's very populated *Freire del Fuego* section of town – Harper Rowe kicked the side of the dresser he was leaning against. "I can think of roughly thirty-eight things that are just grotesquely wrong with this scenario, and roughly *zero* things that are right with it!"

"This is the part where I'd usually say, 'I can think of one thing that's right with it – me!" Devereaux smiled a big, exaggerated smile, "but even I'm not feeling right about being here at this point."

"Can we just do a quick recap on this whole tragic charade?"

"Do we have to?"

"I think it's important to remind ourselves that even though we don't know what's going on here – it seems almost certain that no one else does either."

"Okay, here we go. Number one: someone sets up a sting to catch Black Ice in the act, and apparently they use real bait to do it. She performs a very intricate break-in at the Under Secretary of Defense's house around 7:30 p.m. Ice breaks into the safe on the residence's second floor and that's when we walk in on her. Number two: Black Ice and an accomplice take the contents from the safe and flee out the nearest window where we follow in close pursuit. Number three: we kill all the good guys and let the bad guys get away but only because we were uninformed – our bad – but *we* have seen this woman—"

"*I've* seen her," Harper corrected his partner. "Technically, I saw her. You just lied about seeing her because you're a good friend and didn't want to see me left out there hanging on my own."

"Yeah – technically. Anyway, because of our supposed *face-to-face*"—Devereaux quoted Secretary of Defense Paul Michaels— "with Black Ice, we get sent down here to find her and get the stolen merchandise."

"Correct," agreed Harper and continued on down the list of the previous night's events. "Number four: we get told that we will be working in association with a team of DEA agents in Mexico City. A team that had been totally wiped out almost forty-eight hours prior to all this – and General Higgins knew it, too, because SOD Michaels specifically referenced Chase's heroism and courage from the last 72 hours. He had to've been talking about all of Chase's guys getting wiped out because I'm pretty sure that even with the world's greatest intelligence capabilities, Michaels wouldn't have gotten any information as of yet about our narrow escape from the cartels at the airstrip earlier this morning. I will say that our new partner was quite impressive with her driving skills, to be sure. She probably saved our lives back there."

"Right, but stay focused because here's where it gets tricky. Number five: we fly here early this morning where we are met upon arrival by drug cartels that are under the control of Tito del Fuento. No one seemed to think that this was a likely scenario because they never bothered to tell us that we were going to be getting shot at as soon as we stepped off the flippin' plane!"

"Judas Priest, Kin. Keep your voice down, will ya, Sam? Chase is going to come back here and wonder what the heck is going on." Harper took a seat on the bed next to his buddy. "You're right though. We were pretty close to being done before we ever got started. I don't know – like – somebody tipped off the cartel guys about our arrival, and might have been the same someone that tipped off Chase's DEA raid from the other night."

"Hey," Kin snapped his fingers in front of Harper's face, "stay focused. Number six: we meet up with the heroic and courageous Agent Laurie Chase, who seems completely oblivious to who we are and why we're here. A few minutes later, she proves her worth to us by performing some crazy-good evasive driving techniques." Devereaux stopped for a moment and solemnly lamented, "Ya know, I feel about forty-two different kinds of sorry for that girl. It seems painfully obvious to me that she is in so far over her head on this one."

"Yeah, makes ya wonder why Secretary Michaels has decided to put her in charge on this."

"Number seven: we arrive back here to the flophouse where Secretary of Defense Paul Michaels calls our new friend, puts her in charge, lies to her repeatedly, yells at her for asking stupid questions, and is just, in general, a real jackass to her."

"He definitely lied to her about the circumstances of last night's break-in, that's for sure," Harper continued with the narrative. "Conveniently skirted around how the sting operation went horribly wrong, *but,* since that's entirely our fault that it did go wrong, he probably did save us a little bit of face there. Still, I just can't connect the dots in any way, shape, or form as to what kind of scenario makes sense for the Secretary of Defense of the United States of America to be calling a wounded bird DEA agent and putting her in charge of—"

"Is that number seven or number eight?"

"Hold up," Devereaux interrupted Harper as he pulled his cell phone from the front pocket of his pants. He looked at it inquisitively, and then happily. "Hey, it's Kelly."

"Then I shall take this as my cue to exit stage left. I'll go up front to see what kind of plan Laurie Chase is concocting while you two love birds get re-acquainted with one another. Turn down your com, too. I don't want to be hearing whatever it is you guys are going to be saying to each other. Oh, and be sure to tell Kelly Campbell that I remember that hug she gave me last night at the Under Secretary's house, and I'll be filing a sexual harassment suit against her any day now." Harper gave a congenial, good-hearted smile to his buddy and playfully smacked him on the shoulder as he walked by.

Oblivious to Harper's grandstanding, Kinley answered his cell phone with a good deal of optimism, "Hey, Kelly! Man, am I ever glad to hear from you."

"Oh my god, Kinley, is that really you?" she answered with exasperation. "Where *are* you?" And without waiting for an answer she said, "I need you!"

"Whoa, whoa, whoa, Kells, calm down a little bit. Yeah, it's really me. Harper and I are in Mexico City. What is it that's got you so spooked?"

Kelly was trying to stay composed, but with each word she spoke, she became more unglued. "Gerald and his family – oh, dear God – they're all dead! And that man you were with last night – General Higgins – he's dead, too!"

Devereaux was looking in a wall mirror, amazed at how bloodshot his eyes were. But when Kelly Campbell said the names of Gerald Lange and General David Higgins, he lost track of his surroundings and started paying attention to Kelly's plea. "Kinley, you have to tell me what to do!"

"Do you still have that phone that I gave you about two years ago? The one that I told you to always hold on to and never let out of your sight?"

"Well, yeah, but I just thought—"

"Hang up and go get it. Do it now, Kelly. Call me right back on it."

"It's going—" but before she could even finish her sentence Devereaux disconnected the phone conversation.

Just 30 seconds earlier he had no idea as to the rhyme or reason why any of the events of the last 24 hours were taking place. Until now.

Now Devereaux had some semblance of an idea what was going on.

In a matter of minutes, Kelly called back on the designated phone. Kin answered it on the first ring, "Kelly, tell me again who they found dead. Was one of them a man named Steve Robbins?"

"Yeah, that sounds right. I'm pretty sure one of the men was named Steve Robbins. I don't know how many of them there were. Seems like there were six or seven. I'm so scared right now, Dev. I just don't know what to do. I'm so scared."

"Do you have anyone that you can trust? I don't mean a little. I mean a lot. Your mom, maybe? Some other relative, perhaps? You need to get up with someone and disappear. The sooner the better. We're all in serious danger. I'd tell you why I'm in Mexico City, but I get the feeling the less you know the better off you'll be. Keep track of that burner phone. From here on out it will be our only means of communication. Also, do you have a keyfob that starts your car automatically while you're still inside the house?"

"Yes," Kin could hear the fear in her voice.

"I'm going to need you to go get that and start your car, and if I were you, I'd duck down first and ask questions later." He heard her making her way around her place, a slight moment of silence was followed by a squealing shriek, and then a sigh of relief. "Nothing happened."

"Hit it again, Kels, and make sure you are well clear of where your car is – in a back room maybe."

"Okay."

Kinley could hear her footsteps moving quickly down the hall, her breaths becoming shorter and faster. Breaths that were filled with fear and anxiety.

"Okay, I'm all the way at the back of my house. Here goes—" The call was disconnected immediately. Devereaux tried to call her back but every call went straight to voicemail. The assassin shoved his phone in his pocket in frustration.

Harper Rowe made friends with relative ease on his own without the need of introductions or happenstance. He could talk to anybody about anything and sound good doing it, too. So when he walked to the front of the DEA flophouse and saw Agent Laurie Chase sitting in her dark office with a 3-D hologram of the Mexico City skyline laid out before her, he knew this was a woman he wanted to get to know better. It was no secret that Harper loved gadgets and toys and all things hi-tech, but he had only seen things of this nature on television and in magazines. He watched her manipulate the buildings, and the shapes and sizes that they came in. She seemed to be magically moving things that were not even there just by the simple motion of her hands. It was as if Agent Laurie Chase were a conductor, and Mexico City her orchestra. With child-like amazement, Harper stayed quiet for a few moments as he watched her play about the electric diorama.

"Is that the entire city you have there?"

Slightly startled, Chase looked up from her work to see Harper strolling into her office. "No, this is just a small segment from over in the Colonia de Polanco district. I see you found a suitable shirt. How's your face feeling?"

"It makes me wince every time I blink, but nothing I can't

get my plastic surgeon to take care of when I get back home. I hear he's been looking for a reason to use that power sander he got for Christmas. So, what's up with all of this? I mean, what are we looking at here? And why?"

"Where's Mr. Devereaux? We need to discuss some things. I've just been given new updates about the situation."

"I think he's in the back sweeping the place for listening devices and bugs. I'm also pretty sure that he stumbled onto a vintage collection of Wayne Newton albums still on vinyl. Exactly how old is this place, Agent Chase? I think I saw an etching in the bathroom that was made by Methuselah's father. Doesn't our government even offer a quality maid service to our agents in third world countries?"

"I don't think Mexico is considered third world, Mr. Rowe," Chase said with a peculiar smile.

"Have you looked outside your windows, Laurs? Can I call ya *Laurs*? Have you seen the poverty and desolation and fear in the eyes of the people that are walking up and down these streets? Yeah, this particular city might have some skyscrapers and parks and statues and a few museums, but there isn't anything but death and corruption in this town. The sooner I can get out of here, the happier I'll be."

Harper paused for a moment and then went on, "Yeah, you're right, kid. Mexico isn't looked at as a third world country. It's looked at as the big sandy-brown elongated crap that Texas is taking on Guatemala, and there's not enough toilet paper in the world with which to clean up this mess."

"You're so eloquent." Agent Chase said without any passion. She was completely engrossed in the hologram that lay before her. She was studying the streets, back alleys, air paths, surrounding buildings, and anything else that might be able to give her insight how to use the twin towers and the surrounding skyscrapers in Polanco to her advantage. She had not looked at Harper since he was halfway through his diatribe about Mexico City. She figured he was someone that liked to talk just for the sheer delight of hearing his own voice.

"So, since Kinley's going to be a while doing his thing, I was just wondering if you could show me how this little illuminated hologram gizmo of yours works."

"Harper." Kinley's voice crepitated in Harper's ears. "I need you to politely excuse yourself from the scene and get back here. It's of an urgent nature."

Since Laurie Chase had not bothered to respond to Harper's request, the assassin had no trouble excusing himself from the conversation. He started to rub his stomach lightly and, even though Chase was not looking at him, made a bit of a sour face. "Uh, I think we're going to have to hit the pause button on this for a few. Feels like something I ate on the plane is starting to back up on me a bit."

"Take your time."

"Hurry up." Kinley recapitulated.

"Coming, Mother," Harper murmured under his breath as he strode quickly down the hall toward his partner. "What the heck is going on that's so important, anyway?" At this point the cantankerous Rowe re-entered the back bedroom.

Devereaux was quick to shut the door behind his friend, and in the frankest of manners said, "They're killing everyone that knows about this, Harper. They killed Gerald Lange. They killed General Higgins. All the men that were in the room with us at the Pentagon last night? Dead. I can't help—"

"Whoa, whoa, whoa, man. Did Kelly just tell you all this?"

"Yeah, she did – as her very own vehicle was being blown to shreds in her garage. Whoever took out Lange, Higgins, and their crew had Kelly on their list, as well. Gotta figure that you and I aren't too far down that manifest, either."

Harper took a few brief steps around the room and ran his hands through his close-cut wavy hair in exasperation. "Who is doing this?"

"Don't know *who* – just know *that*."

Harper flashed Kin a bothersome look. "What the heck does that even mean?"

"It means that I don't know *who* is doing the killing, just *that* someone is doing the killing."

"Well, what's going on with Kelly then? Is she okay? I mean,"— Harper sat down on the bed— "is she okay?"

"I talked her through it as best as I could. She's a thousand miles away – and I don't mean to sound like a heartless prick – but she's not really my main concern right now, ya know?"

"Yeah, I hear ya. We need to figure out what our next play's gonna be here."

"You said you've got papers, right? So, worse comes to worst, we got a trap door to escape through, yeah?"

"Yeah, worse comes to worst."

Kinley could hear in Harper's voice that he was starting to panic, and he could see by the rueful look on Harper's face that it was starting to sink in just what an impact his jejune actions from the previous night were now having on everyone around him.

"Did I do all of this?" Harper asked. "Did I get Lange, and Higgins, and all those other men killed because of what I did last night?"

"Be that as it may – what's done is done. If we're going to get out of this we've got to treat it just like any other assignment. Yeah, they might tell us what to do and where to do it, but – bottom line – once we're in the field doing our thing, there isn't anybody there to wipe the spit off of our chins or hold our hands when we cross the street. We are on our own. This is no different. We've got our assignment, and we're going to bring it to its fruition. We are going to find Black Ice, we're going to get whatever it is that she has stolen that's caused all of this chaos, and we're going to see where it takes us, and if there's any possible way to come out of this clean – good Lord, if there's any way to come out of this *at all*, then we're going to do it."

Harper nodded his head in acknowledgement of what his friend said. "Agreed – and since it looks like no one else seems to have any reservations on the body count in this grand-scale catastrophe, I'd say it's time that we start playing by *their* rules."

"I'm excited."

"What about Chase? How do you want to handle her?"

"With kid gloves. Let her be 'in charge' and run the show. Hopefully, she'll be open to input from me and you if we see she's doing something galactically stupid."

"How old do you think she is, Agent Chase?"

"Oh, I don't know," Kinley squinted his eyes in thought for a moment. "A job like she does ages a person in dog years so even though she kinda looks mid-thirties to me, guess it wouldn't really surprise me any if she was in her late-twenties. Why do you ask?"

"Just wondering how thick that skin of hers really is. She seems to have a genuine dislike toward me, that's for sure. I'm thinking that for the time being it's probably best if the kid gloves we handle her with are on your hands."

A sudden loud knock came on the bedroom door. "Are you two going to be much longer because we've kinda got some time sensitive work that needs to be done out here."

"Speak of the devil—" Harper started.

"And the devil appears," Devereaux finished, as he opened the door to see Agent Laurie Chase's solemn face there to greet him. She looked at Kinley and then at Harper, the latter with a bit more disdain than the former. "Are we ready?"

"Yeah, let's do this," Harper said as he bounced up off the bed and trailed Chase and Devereaux up the hallway and back to Chase's office.

TRUST

Although Tara Madison and Desmond Timms did not trust each other, they trusted the situation enough to know that neither of them was any good without the other. This, compounded with extreme exhaustion, caused them to decide their next best move was to get some sleep.

They both lay on the motel bed – Madison under the covers on the side closest to the door, Timms on top of the covers on the side next to the wall.

"You sure you don't want to get under the covers with me, Des? I promise I won't bite," Madison said, feigning enticement.

"If I thought for a minute you *would* bite, I'd certainly entertain the idea, but things bein' what they are, it's definitely in both our best interests to keep this strictly professional."

Tara jerked her head in Timms's direction and snapped her teeth shut loudly. Through a tired giggle she said, "Mmm – kink-kay," then she rolled over, pulled the covers up over her shoulder, and was asleep in thirty seconds.

Desmond Timms drifted off to dreamland a few moments later.

❄ ❄ ❄

Katie Holt was still very much in the dark as to where she was. For the moment, she sat in a 10 x 10 room with no windows and one door, awaiting someone to bring her a phone so that she could make arrangements to be picked up.

Picked up from where? She had no original clue.

The door to the space swung open abruptly and a man wearing a guard's uniform entered carrying her cell phone. He tossed it to Katie then turned and shut the door.

"You got someone you can call?" he asked amiably.

"Yeah," she answered. "Just don't know where to tell them to come pick me up, is all."

"I'm gonna drive you down to the bus stop on the corner of Buena Vista and Latin Drive. Do you know where that is?"

"Oh yeah," she said, somewhat surprised that she was so close to home. Ever since she woke up in this place a few hours ago, it felt like she was a million miles from anywhere. As she pressed a few buttons on her phone to get to her "contacts" screen, Katie felt both disappointed and lucky at the same time. She felt disappointed that she had to give up the information that was going to jeopardize the well-being of the man of her dreams. On the other hand, she felt very lucky to have her cell phone in her hand and to be able to call someone to pick her up and take her back to life as she knew it, when just a short time ago she thought she was looking at some serious prison time.

Sadly, the *last* thing Katie felt was the precision sharpness from the steel blade of a knife as it ran from the left to the right side of her throat in less than a quarter of a second. She dropped her cell phone to the floor and clutched the gaping wound in her neck, but there was nothing that she could do. It was over for her just that fast.

Katie did not even have to time to feel the fear that most people have rush upon them when faced with the sudden realization that they will be leaving this world and heading into the great hereafter.

She slumped forward, exhaled one last breath, and came to her final resting place face down on the tabletop. The guard lifted Katie's body out of the chair and lowered it to the floor. He then opened the door of the room to allow admittance to the sanitization crew that was waiting patiently in the corridor.

"Clean up on aisle five, gang."

*   *   *

Agent Laurie Chase had her hologram of the Polanco skyline pulled up and ready to go as the trio walked back into her office. She had set up two chairs, one for each of the assassins. Devereaux immediately started checking over the layout, looking at each building closely and carefully from every angle as if intent on looking through the windows of the buildings to see if there were, actually, little people moving around inside. "Nice toy," the older of the two assassins commented.

"Well, when you're finished checking out my toy, I have the information that we've been waiting for, and we're going to have to act fast. The stolen contents will be out in the open tonight. The woman that you two, according to Secretary of Defense Paul Michaels, let get away last night will be with them, as well."

Harper smiled when Agent Chase dropped the name of Paul Michaels as if it were supposed to make him and Kinley go all agape with wonderment, so – he did.

"Secretary of Defense Paul Michaels, did you say?" *The* Secretary of Defense Paul Michaels? When did you talk to him?"

"Yes, *the* Secretary of Defense Paul Michaels, and he called about 15 minutes ago to give me the skinny on what is going on, and what we need to do to make it right. He also told me about your run-in with Black Ice last night. How is it you got so close to her, and yet she slipped right through your fingers? Oh dear, that is a shame." Chase's voice had taken on a very irreverent tone. "Ya know, for as much as you run your mouth, Mr. Rowe, I'm surprised you left that part of the story out."

"Well, I had to leave something for the sequel."

"He did say that you two are very good at what you do, although he was rather vague about what that is exactly."

"So, you're saying the Secretary of Defense, of the United States, called you – here – just a few minutes ago?"

"Yes, Mr. Devereaux. Do try to keep up, please. We've got a lot of ground to cover here and a very short time frame in which to do it. We don't need to be wasting time by unnecessarily rehashing points that I feel I have made very clear."

"Okay, two things: first of all, really going to need you to drop the attitude, Peppermint Patty. Second of all, Mr. Rowe and I will stop wasting time when you start making sense. I mean, seriously, in what world is there any logical explanation for one of the most powerful men on the planet to be calling *you*?" Kinley asked pointedly. "I don't mean any offense by that, but come on."

"Oh, I don't know, Kin," Harper went on, "I mean, why wouldn't the Secretary of Defense call her? I, personally, find her to be extremely intelligent and charming, and just an utter delight to be around."

"I guess when you step into a pile of crap the size of what you two stepped in last night, it's going to take a pretty big pooper scooper to clean up the mess. A Secretary of Defense sized pooper scooper. That would be the world where this would make sense," Chase chided. "What is it that you guys have gotten yourselves – and me – into? Believe me when I tell you that the significance of someone with the power of the United States Secretary of Defense calling me directly is *not* lost on yours truly."

"All right. Then let's stop busting each other's balls here and get down to what needs to be done. The Secretary of Defense called you and what did he say?"

While the two men already knew what Paul Michaels had told

her, they also knew that this would be a good way to gauge how dependable Laurie Chase was going to be in this whole deal. If she gave them the straight dope on the conversation with Michaels then it would go a long way for them trusting her. However, if she decided to give them her own version of the exchange between herself and the secretary then it would make for some seriously disturbing reliance issues from here on out.

"He said that he would be dealing with us directly. Actually, he said that he would be dealing with me directly. He wants me to run point on this. Are you two gonna have an issue with that?"

"No," Harper answered. "You know this town a lot better than we do. You're definitely better suited to run point on this than we are."

"We're at your command, Agent Chase."

"Very good. Now here's the basic layout of things." She moved closer to the holograph of the Polanco skyscraper-filled skyline. "According to the information that the Secretary relayed to me, the woman that you two came face to face with last night will be out in the open at approximately 10:00 - 10:30 p.m. local time tonight. She, and possibly some other associates, have set up a meeting on this building here, the Sante Fe East Tower"—she pointed to the top of a tall skyscraper that sat parallel to another tower of the exact same proportions— "where they intend to sell the package to the highest bidder."

"Did Secretary Michaels say what it was that had been stolen? What it is that we're trying to recover?"

"No. He was rather close-mouthed about that. Regardless, he says that the package is our number one imperative. Black Ice and anybody else we can get in the process is just icing on the cake."

"And then what?"

"What?"

"After we get the stolen merch back, what are we supposed to do with it?"

"We didn't really cover that, either. We're going to take this one step at a time, I guess. Right now, he wants us to come up with some semblance of a plan of attack, and then I'm supposed to call him back to fill him in on it so he can give us all the support he can."

"So, do you trust him? Secretary Michaels, I mean?"

"He's the Secretary of Defense. Of course I trust him. Why wouldn't I?"

"Just seems like for such an important matter of national security he sure does seem to be keeping a pretty tight stranglehold on the information he's sending our way." Harper took a seat in one of the chairs that Chase had set up for him and Devereaux. "If it's such an urgent crisis, then why have they sent three relatively novice field agents to do a job that is best left to someone that's got a lot more experience in these things than we do? And if things are in such a state of panic that Paul Michaels is dealing with us himself from up on high in Capitol City then why all the cloak and dagger on the 411?"

Laurie Chase did not offer an immediate answer. She stared intently at the miniature city that was lit up in front of her.

"One last question before we start in on our plan of action." Kinley paused for a second before asking, "Do you trust *us*?"

Again, Laurie chose silence before answering. "Do I have any choice?"

"Well, I'm a firm believer that people always have a choice. It's just that this particular time if you decide to not trust us then there's really not much of a chance of us coming out clean on the other side of this."

"Kin's right. If we don't trust each other implicitly on this we may as well pack up our things and head to St. Petersburg to see the Alexander Nevsky Monastery. The Russian monks there may give us protection, and even if they don't, it's quite the beautiful place to die."

Laurie was quiet for a moment longer, but then with a surprising amount of sincerity she said, "Yes, I will, unequivocally, trust you." She looked at Harper. "Both of you."

"Then let's stop bandying about like a bunch of henpecked school kids and get a plan together, gang."

Skyscraper City

Secretary of Defense Paul Michaels sat at his desk idly looking over some reports to pass the time. He was waiting anxiously for the return phone call from Laurie Chase to update him on how things were progressing in Mexico City.

The intercom on his phone beeped, and the voice of his secretary, Linda Powell, crackled through. "Mr. Secretary, the President is on line one for you, sir. Says it's of an urgent matter."

"Thank you, Linda." Michaels reached over to his phone and slapped the "Line 1" button with his index finger. "Mr. President, what can I do for you today, sir?"

"Paul, what the hell is going on?" The President's tone was short and harsh. "We've got dead bodies all over the place. We've got a huge firefight at Doug Hopkins' house last night. We've got high ranking officials turning up dead about every hour on the hour. Plus, I've got the press breathing hard down my back, and I've got nothing to tell them. So, what you can do for me is to start giving me some straight answers. Right here. Right now."

"Yes sir, Mr. President. Here's what our intel has for us right now. Things have been sketchy from the get-go, but apparently an international thief that goes by the alias of Black Ice broke into the

Hopkins' residence last night during a big political fundraising party and stole some documents that were in an upstairs safe. We were almost able to apprehend her, but she had two accomplices that came to her aid and helped her escape."

"So, this Black Ice – she's a woman?"

"Yes sir, that is correct."

"Do we know where she is now, Paul?"

"We have her tracked to Mexico City, and we have solid intelligence that she is going to be selling the stolen contents tonight at 10:30 p.m. CDT. I have people there on the ground now, sir, and we are implementing a plan to get Black Ice and the stolen contents back to U.S. soil immediately."

"What about her two accomplices? Do we have any idea who or where they are at this time?"

"Again, the details are sketchy, but it would seem that her two accomplices are named Kinley Devereaux and Harper Rowe. We have them down as two assassins-for-hire. They work for the highest bidder."

"Do you think that these are the two men responsible for all of the murders between last night and today?"

"Mr. President, I can't say for sure, but in my heart and in my head, I feel that to be an accurate statement."

"These pricks must have some set of balls hanging from their Christmas tree. Killing a highly decorated 5-star general, one of the top guys I've got over there at the NSA, and some of the best European intel analysts I've ever worked with." The President hesitated for a few seconds.

"Mr. President? Are you still there, sir?"

"Yes, Paul, I'm still here. I'm going to call the cabinet together so we can figure out what's going on here, and what our next best plan is going to be – figure out what we can give the press to keep them at bay for a few hours. Let's see, it's a little after 1 p.m right now. I'll call the meeting for 2 p.m. So don't be late and bring every piece of information that you've got on this."

"Mr. President. I'd like to ask you to give me a little bit of time. I feel like I can have what you will need within the next 24 hours. Hold your presser, but stall for a bit. I'll have Devereaux and Rowe dead to rights by then. We'll have our guys, I assure you, Mr. President." And with that, the Secretary of Defense reached up and disconnected the call. "I wouldn't want to miss this one for the world."

* * *

Harper sat in his chair and Kinley opted to stand while Laurie Chase circled the holograph of the city. "Okay, see these twin towers right here?" she asked, pointing to the middle of the city. "These are the Polanco Twin Towers. This one here is the east tower. This is where they will be, according to what we know: the Santa Fe East Tower."

"And you said that they were going to get this going sometime around 10:30 tonight?" Kinley asked.

"Yes, that is what we know."

"What kind of building is that, the Polanco Twin Towers? I mean, it seems like an odd place to hold a big illegal meeting like that, ya know."

"They're hotel complexes, and at night they're about 60% full at this time of the year. Summertime, no one wants to vacation in Mexico City. It's not a big tourist attraction if you get what I mean. However, if you can get the palm of the right guy greased just the right way, you can get full access to the building and come and go as you please. If I had to guess, I'd say that they'll have people on the ground to make sure no one gets in without proper clearance. They'll have other people all around the perimeter of the building to watch for any problems with unwanted authorities or uninvited guests showing up. They'll have the inside secured so no one goes up or down without being thoroughly searched. My guess is that there's going to be a group of buyers there from all over the world, plus their entourages. Compile that with all the security that will be demanded – I think the roof is probably the only place that can hold all of them."

"What do you have in mind as far as a plan, Agent Chase?"

"Well, getting them on the ground before they go up to the roof is probably right out. They'll have too much security for just the three of us to be able to jump them, grab the contents and make a run for it."

"Yeah – that is right out."

"What about beating them to the spot?" she asked. "I mean, what if we could get to the roof before they did? Maybe set something up like a surprise ambush?"

"Unless you've got some more people that we can use, a surprise ambush will only serve to get us killed. Let's say they've got 30 armed people. If we ambush them that would mean we would have to kill 10 people each before they could get any of us. My best guesstimate is that we would maybe get 3 or 4 each before it was all over for us."

"I've got an idea," Kinley said. He walked around the display of the city and studied it very carefully. "Right here," he pointed to a tall building that was to the east of the Polanco Twin Towers. "How far away is this building from our towers?"

"That's the Merida Building. It's a huge hotel – one of the biggest in the city. It's probably around a half-mile away from the Bosque."

"And how wide is the space between the two Polanco towers? The west one to the east one?"

"About 55 yards or so. Not too terribly far. Why, what are you thinking?"

"Are you a good shot, Agent Chase?"

"Top of my class at West Point."

"What about in the field? Ever had the opportunity to shoot anyone in a live ammo fight?"

"Yeah, a few times. Nothing too recent though."

"Whatchoo got cookin' in that noodle of yours, Kin?" Harper asked.

"Give me a minute," he said crouching down in front of the hologram, running his fingers from building to building. He stood up and cocked his head sideways and continued running his fingers from rooftop to rooftop. He then looked at his partner. "I think I might have an idea."

Harper noticed that Kinley was standing right behind a skyscraper that rose just above the assassin's waistline. "Hey, Kinley, are you standing behind a skyscraper – or are you just really glad to see me?"

"Are you serious?" Chase said, frustrated at Harper's apparent lack of concern for the situation at hand.

"What? When am I ever going to be able to use that line again? Like – never."

"Just concentrate for a minute here, Harper. Here's what I'm thinking: I'm going to position myself here – on the top of the Merida building. Agent Chase, I want you to be over here on the roof of this building—"

"That's the Torre del Burcco building."

"Can you get up there? Can you shoot from there?"

"I don't know. Can't say that I've ever tried."

"Well, you're going to try tonight. So, you'll be shooting from there at a 45 degree angle to the Towers, and I'll be shooting from the Merida building at a 45 degree angle to the Towers. This way we're not shooting at each other. Once everyone's up on the roof, we're going to start picking them off. First, we'll identify which ones have guns and take them out as fast as we can."

"Yeah, but how are we going to get the stolen goods if you two are shooting from other buildings? It's not like you're going to be able to kill everyone, and then the plans are just going to be laying there for us to come along at our convenience and pick them up."

"Harper, you my good man, are going to be up on top of the west tower."

"There's probably going to be security on the surrounding rooftops, Kin. It's not like I'm just going to walk right up there and – well – what am I doing up there again?"

"Don't worry about security or gunmen up on the roof. I'll have your back on this one, brother. What I want you to do is get up on that west tower roof, and when the time is right, shoot a zipline across to the east tower. Agent Chase and I are going to have that place pinned down tighter than a speedo on a Sumo wrestler."

"Wait – what? Shoot a zipline across? What's that going to do?"

"It's going to get you from the west tower over the east tower, is what it's going to do. Unless you think that you can grow a set of wings in the next 8 hours or something."

"Are you making jokes in an attempt to hide the fact that your plan involves me *dying*?" Harper asked in horrid realization. "Although don't think for a second that I don't appreciate the gesture."

"Hey, you're the one that is always going on and on about how you like to kill up close," Devereaux argued.

"Yeah, I like to kill up close. I certainly don't want to be *killed* up close. Big difference there, chum!"

"This is the way it has to be. Unless Agent Chase has some cards hidden up her all-too-revealing sleeves, it's just the three of us, and I'm using what we have to the best of our abilities."

Harper looked at DEA Agent Laurie Chase and realized for the first time that she was wearing a short-sleeved white tee shirt that completely revealed her arms from her shoulder all the way down to her fingertips.

"What about your bra?" Harper asked, grasping for straws at this point, "I heard that from time to time women hide things in their bras."

Chase grabbed the inside of her tee shirt and pulled it down to reveal the cleavage of a very ample bosom. "Full house in here, champ. No room for any tricks."

"So – you two get to take pot shots from just outside Neverland, and I get to take a one-way flight straight into the teeth of hell. Anybody care to give me a ride to the airport?"

"I know you want a second shot at Black Ice, Harp. This is probably the only way you're going to get it. I promise you that Chase and I are going to be blasting everyone we can get a bullet into straight off that roof, partner. Are you going to be willing to do this or not?"

Harper pursed his lips together and breathed heavily through his nose. "What is this – like – Saturday night, right?"

"Yeah, it's Saturday."

"Hmmm. There's never anything on TV on Saturday night, so, what the heck? I got nothin' else to do. Sure, count me in."

Agent Chase looked at Devereaux and said, "Why do I get the feeling that if there were something on TV, he may not be coming along?"

"Oh, I don't know. Maybe because you're smart and perceptive."

"So, I'm going to call the Secretary and inform him of what we have planned."

"No!" both Harper and Kinley said loudly and at the same time.

"You don't want to do that," Devereaux followed up quickly.

"Why not?"

Kin and Harper looked at each other. "Go on, Kin. She seems to like you. She'll probably take this better coming from you rather than from me."

"What?" Laurie Chase asked confused. "What are you talking

about? Why don't you want me calling the Secretary of Defense?"

"As best we can tell, he's the one behind all of this. Whatever his agenda was – or is – he has been taking out people left and right. We know of at least seven, with an attempt on an eighth. To our knowledge, we may be three of the last four people alive that even know what's going on. The fourth being Black Ice. If he knows that we will all be within earshot of the Polanco Twin Towers tonight, he could send some sort of off the grid air attack to blast us into the basement of Mexico City. Secretary of Defense Paul Michaels – he's the bad guy in all of this."

Laurie Chase's face turned pale white as all of the blood drained from it. "No. No, you're both wrong. He's the Secretary of Defense of the United States of America. He's not some kind of terrorist. You two are so far out in left field that you don't even know what you are talking about."

"It's true that we're out in left field," Harper spoke up, "but it doesn't make anything that Kin said any less true. Michaels is chalking up bodies like Pol Pot on Cambodia voting day."

"The guy's bad news, Laurie." Kinley continued. "Call him, tell him whatever you need to – just don't tell him the truth."

"Then what am I supposed to tell him? I'm open for suggestions."

Devereaux looked at Harper for something – anything. Harper gave his friend an indistinct hand gesture and a blink of his eyes which made Devereaux answer, "Tell him that Harp and I got a tip. We figured out where Black Ice is, and we are going to get her. We cut you out, so you have no idea where we are. Tell him, and stick to it, Laurie. Can you do that?"

"You say these things like I'm just supposed to forget that he represents what is good with this country, and the two of you are a couple of strangers that just showed up in my life – uninvited, mind you – but you—"

Harper rose from his chair and bluntly but evenly said, "Yeah, that's right. We are uninvited, but since the Secretary of Defense Paul Michaels isn't good enough to be here in his own stead – you're stuck with us. Pay attention, girlie, there is no one here to help you besides us."

"Because the two of you are my knights in shining armor, is that what this is? I should be kissing the ground that you walk on around here since—"

"Oh, I got something you can kiss, right here, lady—"

"Harper. Knock it off. We're not going to argue about this. Not this – not anything, okay?" Kinley gave his partner a stern look, and then to Chase he gave a gentler look. "Agent Chase, you have to realize at some point that there is *nothing* right about this. Harper and I don't belong here. This is, by far, not our forte. We aren't trackers, not secret agents, and as you can tell – we aren't planners."

"True," Chase said reluctantly.

"And then there's you. I know you might be thinking that this is your ticket to the big time. The Secretary of Defense is calling you directly and asking you to be his #1 helper in this whole, sordid affair, but – c'mon – really?"

Chase let Kinley's words sink in a little bit before saying, "You're asking me to turn my back on my country and lie to one of its leading officials."

"No," Harper spoke up. "Lie, yes. Turn your back on your country? Absolutely not. The one that has turned a back to the country is Paul Michaels. He's lied, killed, schemed, and manipulated his way through this whole thing. I don't even know what his endgame is, but I'm pretty sure it doesn't involve any of us being alive."

"So, I lie to him. Tell him some BS story about what we're *not* doing. How does that even help?"

"Whatever this started out as, it's snowballed to the point that whoever was associated with it in any way, shape, or form is dead. How does your lying to the Secretary of Defense help us? It gives us a chance to do the one thing that might possibly keep us alive for a little longer, and that is getting back the stolen contents that Black Ice is going to try to move tonight. If Michaels knows where these contents are going to be – and the fact that the three of us are going to be there – he could just annihilate all of us, wash his hands of it, and go back to life as he knew it."

Throughout the entire three-way conversation Devereaux continuously moved around, studying the 3D holographic layout of Colonia Polanco and the skyscrapers that were adjacent to the Polanco Twin Towers.

"He's waiting for your call. Hesitation at this point will be fruitless," Harper commented. "So, what are you going to do, Laurie?"

"Are there any other options?"

"As far as the outcome? I really don't know. As far as me?" Harper stood up again. "I'm gonna go ahead and go because staying in one place for too long while Michaels has the resources he has—"

"No, Laurie," Kinley said, "there are no other options. You call him and tell him what we asked you to, or we can all part ways right now and begin living out our remaining years scared, off the grid, and useless. Sorry to put the weight of our collective worlds on your shoulders, but the cards have been dealt and it's up to you whether or not we play or fold."

Laurie Chase shut her eyes in thought for just a moment, attempting to wrap her mind around what was being asked of her.

She knew.

She knew that what the two assassins were saying made too much sense to ignore. They did not belong here.

Even more, she did not have any conceivable notion as to why someone with the amount of power that Secretary of Defense Paul Michaels wielded would ever put her in charge of such an issue of national security.

Unless it was for a personal agenda.

"Okay. I'll make the call."

Harper exhaled heavily in relief and plopped back down in his chair. "Hope is alive and well."

"You're doing the right thing, Laurie," Devereaux reassured her. "However, before you call the Secretary to give him the bogus plan, let's go ahead and shore up our real plan."

"Sure. Let's."

Kinley pointed to one of the holographic buildings. "I need to be here. What is this building?"

"It's the Zircon Building. It's an architecture firm – one of the biggest in the country."

"Well, hopefully there won't be too many busy-beaver architects working late on a Saturday night. Because this is where I'll have the best sightline to the rooftop of the Polanco Tower East."

"Wait, I thought you just said that you were shooting from the Merida building."

"Yeah, well, I just did some reconfiguring on my angles and direct lines. This building here – the architect building – this is where I need to be. Agent Chase, you will still be perched atop of the del Burcco building..." He cocked his head slightly as he further studied the layout of the city. "Yeah, these are going to be the best positions for the two of us."

Laurie Chase stepped up to the configuration and pointed to the west tower of the Polanco Twin Towers. "This here is the housing for the heat and A/C for both buildings. And attached to it right here is a large antenna for the wi-fi and satellite TV for the building. Harper, you can climb up on this housing unit, and this antenna array will be more than strong enough for you to anchor your zipline to. And it will also give you the height that you will need to get up enough momentum and speed to make it across to the other tower."

"Well, it's good to know that I will have enough momentum to carry me across into what appears to be certain death," Rowe said, laughing at his own joke.

Chase and Devereaux smiled nervously with him.

"Hey, relax, kids. Let's face it, with my skillset and interminable faith, I really give *me* the best chance at making it out of this whole mess alive."

"I got my money on you, Harper."

"Agent Chase, this is your city. When do you think we should head out to give ourselves enough time to get into place and scope the scene for any and all problems that may arise?"

"Well, I'll drive. I can drop the two of you where you need to be, then I will drive to where I need to be. That will probably take – depending on traffic – about forty-five minutes to an hour. We want to give ourselves plenty of time, so"—Chase bit her lower lip thoughtfully— "we probably need to get out of here in about an hour and a half."

Harper stood up from his chair. "That's all I needed to hear. I'm gonna go take a quick forty-five minute nap."

He headed for the hallway, but then he stopped short and turned around and looked at Chase. "You need to know that at this point all protocols are off. You've never experienced anything like this. Neither have we." He looked at Devereaux, then back to Chase. "It's just the three of us now."

"I get that, and I understand."

Devereaux breathed a sigh of relief. "Thank God."

To which Harper replied, "Good. I'm gonna go thank God myself, and then take a nap. I'm sure the two of you won't need any parental supervision while I'm gone. I'll see ya 'round downtown, kids."

✳   ✳   ✳

While Harper was on his way to get a nap, Desmond Timms was being awakened from a deep sleep by Black Ice calling his name. "Dez, wake up. The phone's for you," she barked. Desmond was a bit irritated because, number one, he was enjoying his peaceful slumber, and number two, Ice had taken the unwelcome liberty of answering his cell phone for him. He snatched it abruptly from her hand. "This is Desmond."

Black Ice motioned for Desmond to move the call to speaker-phone. He complied.

"Desmond, it's Adrik," his voice thick with a Russian accent. "Who's the woman answering your phone?"

Timms gave a disgruntled look at Tara and said, "Just a business associate."

"Well, regardless, I just wanted to give you an update on the security setup for tonight."

"Any hiccups?"

"None," replied Adrik. "We'll have the entire building on lockdown. We'll funnel all the traffic up the stairwell of the building. Gone will be any weapons that they may have thought about bringing. The only ones that will have weapons up there tonight will be our men."

"You have my complete faith, Adrik."

"I even checked the weather to make sure it wasn't going to interfere in any way. Clear skies, my friend."

"That sounds good, Adrik. I hired you because you are the best at what you do, and I've paid you that way, too."

"For which I am truly grateful. FYI, I already have men downtown scouring the rooftops and the streets to make sure we do not have any unwanted voyeurs or party crashers."

"Well, be sure to tell your security team to inform me of any unwanted lookers. This is definitely a hush-hush job. No need to go waking up the neighbors with any unwarranted gunfire."

"You got it, boss."

"Stick close, chief."

"You know I will."

Timms disconnected the call and looked harshly at Ice. "I know we have an agreement, but strangers answering my phone make my people nervous. Don't do that again."

"Fine. Let's get this plan in motion and be done with each other. I'm already souring on you. No offense."

"I'm not real keen on you, either, Ice, but business is business. We need each other for now. We pull this rabbit out of the hat tonight, we go our separate ways, and keep each other in our rolodex for future jobs."

"Yeah, for tonight, you're my best friend. And for what it's worth, I hate hats, but I love rabbits, so don't go getting any stupid ideas once we're on that roof tonight with your security guys, okay?"

"I have no allegiance to anyone, Ice. For me, this is all about the money. The rest of the world can blow themselves up, for all I care. I'll be enjoying the view from some Bahamian beach sipping on a Mai Tai."

THINGS YOU DID NOT KNOW
ABOUT HARPER ROWE

While Harper went to nap, Kinley sat in front of the computer checking the weather forecast. Laurie Chase peered over his shoulder from behind.

"So, your friend seems like a real peach."

"Who? Harper?" Kinley spun around in his chair to face her.

"I don't see any of your other friends hanging out with us." Devereaux laughed.

"What? You all of a sudden enjoy my droll sense of humor?"

"I enjoy your sense of humor, to be sure, but don't make the same mistake that everyone else does. You think that Harp makes jokes about everything as some sort of defensive mechanism. I assure you that is not the case whatsoever. If anything, it's an offensive mechanism because he uses it to get into your head and mess around with you."

Devereaux paused for a moment to let his words sink in, then started again. "He's afraid of heights."

"Bull crap," Chase said incredulously.

"I kid you not. He hates them. This is why he kills the way he does. I swear to you that the kid is a deadly shot, but he hates the height that we shoot from. He loves his country though. You ask him to do something for God and country – he's your best soldier."

"Does he know that he is going to die up on that rooftop tonight? Is he willing to do that?"

"You know that he's going to die, and I know that he is going to die, but I'm pretty sure he's already making reservations for a big breakfast tomorrow morning at the local Denny's."

"Denny's?"

"It's about what we can afford, sadly. Ya know, we kill two to three people a month to ensure the safety of millions. Ya'd think they'd pay us more."

Chase looked at Devereaux perturbed. More jokes.

It did not trip Devereaux up in the slightest. "I don't think it's ever entered his mind – dying tonight. I honestly don't think he cares," Devereaux said sincerely.

"We all have a sense of awareness," Chase said.

"Harper never knew his father, but when his dad died, he went to the funeral. He cried. I asked him why he was crying over a man he never knew. He just said 'It's what we're supposed to do,' and he cried for a man he never knew. I don't know if his dad ever knew how much his stupid jerk of a son loved him. From there, Harper meandered through life until 9/11. When that tragedy happened, he decided it was time to stop meandering and time to do something that would make a difference. Harper joined the military, but, as you can imagine, the military was *not* a good fit for the kid.

"The military loved him because he became a killing machine, but a killing machine with a conscience. The U.S. military takes very seriously the old saying, 'Ours is not to reason why; ours is but to do or die' when it comes to their soldiers. He served in Iraq under a commanding officer that did *not* have a conscience. The guy was giving orders to take out areas that had a lot of non-hostiles mixed in with the hostiles – women and children, etc. Harper watched the men around him turn into animals all in the name of following orders. He wouldn't do it, so he walked. Got a dishonourable discharge and was pretty much disgraced out of the whole shebang."

"I did not realize that you knew him for that long."

"Oh, I didn't. These are just things that I learned from looking into his background and talking to him over the last three years. Although, if you were to look into his background these days, the only thing you would find is whole lot of nothing."

"So, how did he end up doing this? Working for the same country that hung him out to dry and humiliated him for his personal convictions?"

"Well, if there is one thing that Harper is better at than killing, it's compartmentalizing. He sees those people as just a small drop in the bucket of who and what the United States is and for which it stands. He took it upon himself to find out who the war machine was targeting next, and he went and dispatched of them himself. After about three successful kills, he let it be known unto the powers that be that he was responsible for the recent annihilation of these three Middle Eastern tyrannical targets. After that, secret calls were made, behind-closed-doors meetings were held, chips fell, and before too long, Harper was unofficially on the payroll of the United States government."

"Wow. Interesting. Good history lesson," Chase said, "and I'd love to hear more, but it's getting to be about that time – time for the call to the Secretary of Defense of the United States."

"Do it. You know what to say to him, right?"

"I'm learning. It's like the two of you do this every day. I – just so ya know – do *not* do this every day. I'm scared clueless as to what to say or how to act."

"Act like his lackey – act natural. You do know how to act naturally, don't you – while all the time lying through your teeth?"

"Screw you," Chase lashed out.

"That seems harsh," Kinley said. He returned to staring at the computer screen, focusing on the weather. "It's a good night for shooting. The winds are low and the sky is clear. If ever there was hope – we find it in the weather."

✳   ✳   ✳

Tara finished her shower. She grabbed a towel and walked naked back into the hotel room that she and Desmond shared.

She dropped the towel.

"Not interested," Timms said flatly.

"Seriously? You don't want any of this?"

"Can't believe you are trying to knock me off my game like this."

Tara walked over to him seductively and said, "I'm not trying to knock you off your game – just making sure you are still *on* it, is all."

Desmond got dressed.

Tara got dressed.

It was time to go.

It was money-making time.

DOOMSNIGHT PREPARATION

Harper was sleeping like a dog when Kinley pressed his shoulder.

"Wakey, wakey, it's time for eggs—"

"Shut it, Dev. Or you'll be wearing the eggs and bakey as a helmet."

"Feeling a bit grumpy today, are we?"

"I was just having an amazing dream with me and Minnie Driver riding bareback on an elephant down in the Amazon. It was one of those dreams where you're naked, but it doesn't feel off kilter because it's somewhat appropriate. Do you ever have dreams like that, Kin?"

"Yeah, but mine are usually me with Nell Carter, and we're in the middle of the Pacific Ocean in a life raft with an entire family of porcupines."

"Well," Harper wiped the sleepiness from his eyes, "at least, it's not *Jimmy* Carter."

Kinley reached down and gave his friend a hand up off the bed. "Chase is calling Paul Michaels now. She's telling him that we're planning on intercepting Black Ice at street level before she can even get up to the roof to sell the goods. As soon as she's finished, we'll go ahead and link her com in with ours, and we'll officially be a team."

"Oh, can our official team mascot be Fudd Duck?"

"It for sure can be."

"Kin, were you able to find a decent sniper rifle to use tonight? What about the weather? Have you checked that?"

"Yeah, relax, partner. I came across a sweet tricked out M4 that one of the guys on Chase's DEA team had assembled. It is just what the doctor ordered."

"What about a top flight zipline. Were we able to commandeer something like that for me to use tonight?" Harper asked anxiously.

"Harper," Kinley shushed. "We're ready. Okay? I know your mind is moving through your mental landscape around 200 miles per hour right now, but just chill for a minute." Devereaux placed both of his hands firmly on Harper Rowe's shoulders. "We will be fine, brother."

Rowe took a deep breath and exhaled slowly. "We will be fine, won't we."

"Eh, probably not, but it just seemed like the right thing to say."

Secretary of Defense Paul Michaels had just hung up the phone with DEA Agent Laurie Chase when he was paged by his secretary, Linda Powell. "Mr. Secretary, Agent Crool is here to see you."

"Send him in, please."

Before Linda Powell could give him the instruction, Crool opened the door to Michaels's office and stuck his shaved head in. "Secretary Michaels, sir, Agent Jeb Crool reporting as you requested."

"Come in, Agent Crool," Michaels instructed. Crool had not fully entered the office before Michaels began barking out the situation. "Agent Crool, first and foremost, I just want to thank you for your service to your country today. I know you are well aware of the situation that has unfolded in the last 24 hours as far as the national security of our country is concerned. Currently, I have a jet fueled and ready with an entire team of soldiers waiting for your orders. I have a car on its way here to pick you up and take you to that jet." At this point, Crool stood at attention, listening to his commander's instructions.

"And what are those orders, sir?"

"As you have already been privy to this operation, you have some idea as to what is taking place in just a few hours. I have a team of people that are preparing to recover the contents that were taken from the Under Secretary's house last night. With divine intervention and godspeed, the Mexico City team will reclaim the stolen property. What I need you and your team to do is to take possession of the contents from them – and then dispose of the Mexico City team."

"The Mexico City team, sir?"

"Yes, Agent Crool. It is not something that I wish to do. It's a team that we were not able to completely read into this whole operation. We are still not sure of the security clearance that they have. It could be dangerous, Jeb. I do not want to take any chances with something this important. I do hope you understand?"

"Yes sir, Mr. Secretary."

"I would love for you to be able to have an occasion to find out whether or not they were able to meet clearance codes, but, sadly, that sort of thing will not present itself this time around on this mission. Your mission assignment is to take your team, go to Mexico City, get what we need and dispatch of whomever tries to stand in your way. This is the address where they are staying," Michaels said as he extended a folded piece of paper to Agent Crool. "It's a DEA safehouse. I want you and your men to sit on it and wait for them to show up later tonight. If they don't have the thumb drive on them – kill them – and then give me a call for further instructions."

"And if they do have the thumb drive?"

"Your orders are the same either way, Agent Crool."

"Consider it done, Mr. Secretary," and with that, Agent Jeb Crool dismissed himself from Paul Michaels's office.

DOOMSNIGHT BEGINS

Back in the van, Harper, Kinley, and Laurie Chase assumed the same seating arrangement as they had on their way from the airstrip. Agent Laurie Chase was at the helm. Kinley Devereaux was in the passenger seat. Harper Rowe crouched just behind the two of them, between the seats.

The team had scrounged together everything that they thought that they were going to need for tonight's job. Some from the DEA safehouse. Some from the gym bags that Kinley and Harper had packed from the armory on the plane they had flown in on. Some from a local drugstore that they had passed on their way to the Zircon Building.

For Kinley, they had found a very oversized Oakland Raiders jacket which was just big enough for him to strap in all the different parts of his tricked-out M4 assault rifle. Walking down the city streets of Mexico City – especially in the Polanco district – with a sniper rifle case strapped across his back just did not seem like a hot idea to Kinley. The oversized Raiders jacket was a very acceptable alternative. Even though it was the middle of summer, in Mexico City a coat like that was a popular fashion statement any time of the year. He also shouldered a bag containing his sniper's mat and two blankets: one to camouflage himself up on the roof of the Zircon building, and the other to muffle the gunfire of his rifle.

For Harper they had found a way to fit the zipline kit into a decent-sized backpack. He also managed to secure three guns, twelve clips, a hatchet, some piano wire, a stiletto knife, pepper spray, mace, four Chinese throwing stars, three grenades, and a diver's knife to his body in some way, shape or form.

Chase had seen Harper with the three handguns. "I didn't think you liked guns?"

"While they're not my usual preference, I do know when they are the most realistic option." Harper picked up one of the handguns and started wrapping the butt of the gun with double-sided tape.

"Why are you doing that?" Laurie asked.

"When I'm ziplining and running around like a madman on the east tower tonight, the last thing I want to worry about is dropping my weapon. This double-sided tape will help ensure that I don't do that."

"What about fingerprints? Won't that double-sided tape leave a perfect impression of your finger and palm prints all over it?"

"You'd think, but I'm pretty sure the gloves I'll be wearing will take care of that problem," Rowe said sarcastically.

Rowe had also found the one thing that was actually going to be more helpful than any of the weapons he was carrying. It was the one thing he needed to get *off* of the roof.

For Laurie, it was three blankets: one on which to lie, since she did not have a sniper's mat of her own; one for her sniper's rifle, a PSG-1; and a third to cover her from any overseers.

"We'll get to the Zircon Building first, Kinley. We can drop you there. Polanco Towers will be second – I'll drop you there, Harper. I will then take the van to a discreet parking place before I head to the del Burcco Building."

"How far away is the Zircon Building from Polanco Towers?" Harper inquired.

"A little over half a mile. Del Burcco is a bit less than that."

"I'll just get out with Kinley at the Zircon Building then. I'll trek it on foot from there. It'll give you guys time to get in place and scan the other rooftops, and it will give me a chance to see what kind of preliminary security might be down on street level."

"Suit yourself," Chase said. "Besides, I could probably use the quiet to get my mind focused a bit."

"Agent Chase, can you do me a huge favor?" Harper asked. "When you're up on that rooftop tonight, firing your bullets for all you're worth – hit something. I don't care if it's just a flesh wound on someone's butt cheek – just hit *something*."

Laurie looked in the rearview mirror at Harper. "It's killing you that your life is in my hands tonight, isn't it?"

"And sexier hands, they could not be in," Harp smiled.

In owl-like fashion, Kinley Devereaux turned his head slowly, but not the rest of his body, until he fixed his glance on his partner. "You were talking to me, weren't you?"

✳   ✳   ✳

About the time Laurie was dropping Kinley and Harper off outside the Zircon Building, a few minutes past 6 p.m. local time, Agent Jeb Crool and his team took off and began winging their way to Mexico City. There were five men total, including Jeb. Unlike Devereaux and Rowe, who had landed at the private airstrip just outside the city some twelve hours earlier, Crool and his team already had gotten clearance to land at the Benito Juarez International Airport, the biggest and busiest airport in all of Mexico City. Upon landing, the team planned to rent a car and drive to an appointed location to meet up with someone that Secretary of Defense Paul Michaels had slotted to deliver the men the necessary weapons and materials they would need to carry out this assignment.

During the flight, Crool laid out the details of the short assignment as best he could. It was still a little sketchy to him just exactly how things were going to play out since the mission itself could go one of two ways.

"If they have the thumb drive then we're in for a penny. If they don't have the thumb drive then we could be in for a pound. Several of them, actually. Either way, we put the three of them down."

As Jeb said these words to his team he was already wondering if putting down Kinley Devereaux, Harper Rowe, and Laurie Chase meant the same fate may be in the cards for him and his crew. This would not be the first time that following orders meant putting down friendlies. Nevertheless, orders were orders, and since they had come straight from the mouth of his highest ranking superior, he knew that this was one mission from whose path he did not want to alter or stray.

✳   ✳   ✳

Desmond Timms sat in the rental car that he had acquired earlier that morning when he landed at the airport. He was waiting patiently in the parking lot of a bus depot while Tara Madison was inside retrieving the thumb drive. She had put the drive in one of the depot lockers for safe keeping until she needed it for the meeting tonight.

Timms was futzing with the radio, trying to find a station that played American music when Madison opened the passenger side door and got back into the car. She held up the thumb drive and commented, "Hard to believe this little number is going to make us rich beyond our wildest dreams."

"We've come along way on this, Ice. One last hurdle to go, and we'll be set for life. My security man, Adrik, just texted me. They are all in position and ready to go. He also says that he's been scanning the airwaves, and as of yet, no one seems to have a clue as to who is responsible for the massive shooting at the Under Secretary's house last night, nor for the slaying of the six men early this morning at the Hotel Habita."

"I never thought for a moment that they would. I'm not one to leave behind even so much as a scent for dogs to follow. By the time those jackasses figure out what happened, I'll be in a land far, far away – with no extradition laws."

"In a few hours, we'll be nothing but rumours and speculations."

"And to think, I came within an eyelash of getting caught last night."

Timms looked at her somewhat surprised. "What do you mean? Almost got caught? How?"

"Right in the middle of the production last night, we are up in the room, and Kilpatrick cracks the safe, I grab the drive, and then from out of nowhere, these two morons stumble in on us. I shoot at 'em and they recoil back into the hallway, and Kilpatrick and I are outta there faster than a mouse out of a maze, I tell ya. We scale the outer perimeter wall as fast as we can, and start running up the street to my truck to get our asses outta there. Next thing we know, there are guns a-blazing behind us. I hear one shot whistle past my ear, and then they shoot Kilpatrick in the back of his head, and his body comes crashing down on the back of my legs which, in turn, sends me sprawling face-first onto the gravelly pavement. One of the dudes that I shot at in the upstairs room – he's right on top of me. I had to dispose of him real quick and in a hurry. I give him a shot to the groin, roll him off of me, and make it to my truck for a quick exit out of there. I left about ten pounds of rock, stone, and dirt in the poor bastard's face. Once I left there, I did not look back."

"Wow. Someone other than a co-criminal getting a look at the face of the great Black Ice? Any idea who this guy was?"

"No, but he was a cocky little jerk, though."

"Think he can identify you?"

"Are you kidding?" Madison laughed. "The shape I left him

in, he'll be lucky if he can identify himself the next time he looks in a mirror."

"We got a while before we have to be there."

"Let's go get something to eat. I'm starved. Being in that bus station around all those bums – I don't know what it is about the smell of homeless people that always makes me hungry."

Timms gave her the most incredulous of looks, his left eyebrow raised, his nose crinkled to show his teeth. "You ain't right, lady. You ain't even close to bein' right."

Tara giggled an evil giggle. "I suppose it's too much to hope to find a Stuckey's in this town, eh?"

Kinley and Harper stood at street level, staring up at the top of the Zircon building.

"Judas Priest, how high do you figure this building is?" asked Harper, in awe of the magnificent structure.

"Looks like 41 stories, as best as I can tell."

"Holy – moly. How big is the one I'm gonna be on?"

"I think Chase said it was something like 36 stories."

"Oh, thank goodness. I thought it was going to be really tall like this one."

"Trust me, kid," Devereaux laughed, "they look a lot bigger when you're on the top of them. My advice to you? When you hit that zipline tonight – don't look down."

"Oh, there's no need to worry about that, chief. When I hit that zipline tonight, both my eyes are going to be closed in devout prayer."

Kinley laughed. "That's what I love about you, Harper. Even at the eleventh hour, you don't falter or waver a bit."

"Solid to the end."

Kinley gave his friend a tight hug. "Don't die up there tonight, okay?"

"Lotta people gonna die tonight," Harper said, breaking the embrace. He looked Kin right in the eyes and said, "I'll meet you for a drink after they do."

And with that, Harper backpedaled a bit before turning and taking off into a full sprint toward the Polanco Towers.

Roughly ten seconds later Laurie Chase's voice crackled through both of their coms. "Thank God, that's over. I thought I was going to have to listen to the two of you exchanging numbers or something."

Problem #1

When Laurie Chase hit the roof of the Torre del Burcco building, she was glad she had brought the three blankets. The view was amazing, no doubt, but the roof was filthy with oil, bird crap, trash, and who knew what else. Plus, it was cold.

She took the first blanket from her pack, found the best spot on the roof, and laid it down. Next she took the pieces of her PSG-1 out of the bag and deftly assembled the rifle. From there, it was looking through the scope to find the Polanco Towers – both of them – and taking everything that was blurry and just under a half-mile away and making it crystal clear. Once satisfied with her view, she put the second blanket over the top of the muzzle of her weapon, then got into place and pulled the third blanket up over herself. She settled into a good position and said to the duo, "I'm in position. Got the target sighted. Ready to go."

It was silent for a moment. Chase was getting ready to repeat herself when Kinley crackled into her ear. "Same here. Set and scanning."

"Copy that, copycats," Rowe said flatly. "Still on the move to my stop. Probably five more minutes till I'm to my twenty."

Silence for almost two minutes until Laurie said, "Being here under moonlit skies and on a blanket and having two guys hanging on my every word – it's almost romantic."

"Crap," said Kinley.

"Crap?" replied Chase.

"Crap?" echoed Harper.

"Yeah, crap. Harper, don't go up to your rooftop once you get there. I'm spotting four bogeys there right now, as we speak."

"Oh-kay."

"Don't worry, this isn't unexpected. It's very dealable."

"So, you saw this coming?" Harper asked. "Next time do me a favor, Nostradamus, and fill me in, will ya?"

"Chill, kids. It'll be fine. Just a small glitch. Harper, you do your thing with your little key card and just find a place to hole up until it's show time. You can take another nap or think of your next smart alec line or something. When it's go time, I'll take 'em out from where I am."

"What? No. Forget that," Rowe came back.

"Forget what?" Kinley asked.

"Forget taking them out from where you are, Kin. No need to give your position away any sooner than we need to. Once it's go time, I'll take them out – quickly and quietly. Like a deadly church mouse."

"You sure?"

"As sure as I am that Chase is going to say something goofy right now."

"Wow. Seriously," started Chase, "you two should write greeting cards for a living as much as you go back and forth with each other."

Silence.

And then—

"Okay, Harper. You can take them out," said a convinced Devereaux.

READINESS

The flight landed and Jeb Crool and the boys deplaned in Mexico City. The group walked silently to the rental car area of the Benito Juarez International Airport.

As they walked, Crool phoned Secretary of Defense Paul Michaels.

"We've landed. Heading to get the car now. Anything new on your end?"

"No, but I don't expect to hear anything for another hour or so. With something like this, it's hard to say when it will go down. Time – it's what keeps everything from happening all at once."

"Roger, that."

"As soon as I hear anything, Agent Crool, you will be the first to know. For now, get your men to the address I gave you to rendezvous with the weapons contact."

"We'll be on our way in just a few minutes, Mr. Secretary."

Tara Madison and Desmond Timms were finished eating and on their way to the biggest payday of their lives.

Adrik Karismov and his security team were set up and ready to ensure that there were going to be no problems whatsoever with the proceedings tonight.

Jeb Crool and his men had landed in Mexico City and were on their way to get a rental car to ride to the next step of their mission.

Kinley Devereaux and Laurie Chase were set atop their respective rooftops and ready to fire at go-time. They had already spotted the security teams that had been assigned to closer rooftops, and they both had been in contact with Harper Rowe as to what was where.

Then about a half an hour before the main festivities were supposed to start, the two of them – Kinley and Laurie – heard what sounded like rain coming through their coms.

"Harper, what's that noise?"

"I'm taking a shower."

"What?" asked a perplexed Chase.

"Oh, yeah, and it's great. Like an Amazon rainforest, just without all the mosquitoes. Gosh, really wish you guys could be here."

"Harp, what are you doing?"

"Hey, remember when you told me to find a safe place to hole up in, Kin? Yeah, well, I did that. Found this great place on the top floor. No one was in it so I decided to help myself to the amenities that I found herein. Massage bed, sauna – right here in the suite – it was sweet. Lit'rally, a sweet suite. And now I'm taking the best shower ever. Man, I've never been so focused."

"I think I am gonna wing somebody's butt cheeks tonight, Harper," said Chase, "and they're gonna be yours."

"Take it easy, kids. If everything goes south tonight, you two get to run away from it all. I'm the one that goes down in flames. I'm just living my last day to the fullest."

"Get dressed, Harper. It's time," Kinley said, hesitated, and then said, "Time to kill or be killed. Hope you're ready, brother."

Fudd Duck

When Tara Madison walked into the ground floor of the east tower of the Polanco Towers with Desmond Timms, she was very impressed with the way things were being handled. She almost felt like royalty, the way the security team led her to the elevators and escorted her onto them. She and Timms rode the lift all the way to the top floor, and when she exited the elevator she found even more guards ready to escort her and Desmond to the rooftop. Once she opened the door, it was all laid out for her. Representatives from thirty-two different countries awaited her arrival. Each with suitcases full of money.

"Are they unarmed?" she asked her security escort.

"Yes, ma'am. They've all been cleared."

She looked at Desmond, "You really *do* know how to get the job done. I'm impressed."

"Shine me on some other time, Ice. Let's go do some business."

Meanwhile, Harper Rowe was making his way to the top of the west tower.

"You see where I'm coming out onto the roof, Kin? Tell me where the baddies are in accordance with my position."

Kinley was using his ballistic drop compensator, also known as a BDC, to start figuring out the variables that he would have to battle once he started shooting. The BDC was a small round dial that helped the assassin to adjust his scope for environmental and atmospheric irregularities such as wind, barometric pressure, bullet trajectory, etc., once he had his range settings calculated.

Without breaking his concentration, Devereaux said, "You'll come out, and they are all to your right – within ten feet of your entrance."

"Well, keep your sights on me – just in case."

And with that, Harper Rowe sprang onto the rooftop, saw his prey and went after them with the ferocity of a mother tigress. He took one down with a well-placed Chinese throwing star. The next assailant felt the palm of Harper's hand as it smashed into his nose and drove both of his nasal bones into his brain.

Two down, two to go.

For attacker number three, Harper tried to do a spinning roundhouse to the guy's skull, but he missed badly and ended up feeling the force of a kidney punch land in his back. It sent him sprawling.

"Oh, crap," Kinley commented as he took in the entire scene through the high-powered scope on his rifle. "You were doing pretty good up to there."

Harper Rowe recovered quickly and was back to his feet.

"Dude, stop trying to show off and finish them already!" Laurie said from her respective rooftop.

"Fine," Rowe said, a bit disgruntled. He pulled the diver's knife from somewhere on his body. The third attacker – the one that had just knocked Harp on his can – now had a .357 Magnum trained on Harper's head. The gunman laughed and said something in a dialect that even Harper could not understand.

"Hey, Cousin Itt, I'm not sure what you just said, but I hope it was a prayer before dying," and seemingly without moving a muscle, Harper launched the diver's knife right through the guy's chest.

Goon number four thought for sure he would be the one to take

Harper down. He had his gun leveled, trigger finger primed, and was ready to shoot – but before the message could get from his brain to his hand, Kinley Devereaux's sniper bullet from over a thousand yards away permanently retired his number.

"Bogeys down. Tell me what I have," Harper barked as he began to climb up the heating and air conditioning warehousing to the antenna where he was going to anchor his zipline.

"The closest wall where you will be landing is your twelve o'clock. You have guards – four at your twelve," Kinley barked, "three at your three, five and I think our lady at your six, and five at your nine!"

"I'm hooking up and shooting the zipline. No better time than now to start firing."

"Laurie!" Devereaux shouted.

"Stop yelling, Kin, I can hear you."

"Pin the door down," he said a bit more quietly. "Don't let anyone on or off of that rooftop."

And underneath the starlit skies and the tranquility that was far above the buzzing streets of Mexico City, Laurie Chase started firing from her comfy blanket, and Kinley Devereaux started firing from over a half a mile away – it all seemed beautiful and poetic.

"I'm linked up. I fired the zipline, and it seems tight – here goes nothin'." And Harper launched himself.

With his right hand, Harper held tight to the handle that was attached to the zipline. With his left hand he pulled out one of his handguns and started firing at whatever was moving.

"Fudd Duck!"

When that gun ran dry, he shook it loose from his hand, pulled out a second gun and started firing again. That is when he saw her.

Black Ice.

Tara Madison.

The girl that had spun out in his face.

Butt Cheeks and Satisfaction

Harper landed.

The carnage was massive, and the mayhem was even greater.

"Good golly, it looks like Times Square on New Year's Eve up here. I sincerely think that no one even realized I just ziplined in. I'm kind of offended, actually."

"Do you see her?" Laurie asked pointedly.

"I did on my way in, but now that I'm here on roof level, it's just mass chaos. I can't see bupkis from here. Keep that door pinned down, Agent Chase. Do not let anyone off of this roof!"

"I can't see you, Harper," Kinley said. "I'm still firing at targets so keep your head down."

"I'm the one that's not running around like an extra in a Three Stooges short. Don't shoot me."

"Roger that, Harp."

"I think I just winged some guy's butt cheek," Laurie chided.

Harper felt like a ball in a game of bumper pool. He was being run into and jostled about with no concern. He was the chewing gum, and everyone else around him were teeth.

"I see her!"

"Where are you on the—"

"Do what you're doing. It's working. I got this chick in my sights. I got this."

While Laurie Chase was firing away with everything she had to keep the rooftop door pinned down, and Kinley Devereaux was trying to decipher between the armed targets and the targets with just arms, amidst the pandemonium and tumult that was all around him, Harper fought his way through the frenetic crowd like a running back through linebackers until he reached his goal.

He grabbed her.

Tara Madison.

He held her down.

Desmond Timms was right next to her. Timms pulled his weapon to kill Harper, but the assassin was quicker. Harper tossed one of his knives into the gullet of Desmond Timms.

Timms fell.

Timms bled.

Desmond Timms died.

"I can't believe you found me again," Madison said in utter disgust and disbelief.

"Oh, right," cackled Rowe, "as if there was ever any doubt."

She squirmed and slapped at him, trying her best to break free from his grasp. But it was an exercise in futility.

"Stay down, and you might live."

Gunfire was going off all around them. There was blood. There was death. There was mayhem.

"Give me the thumb drive and I'll let you go," he said to Madison.

"No way!" She spit in his face.

"I really have no problem with you at this point, but if you don't give me the drive then I've got a bullet that is ready to personally escort you into the next life."

"Forget you, mother fu—"

"Give it to me!"

"I can't! Okay?" she screamed at him. "Even if I wanted to. It's in the briefcase. I swear."

"You mean the briefcase that is conveniently handcuffed to your wrist?"

"It's in the briefcase, I swear on my life."

"Open it."

"I don't have the key," Black Ice said.

"Not a problem," said Harper, and from out of nowhere he pulled the hatchet.

"What – what are you doing with that?" she asked, panic stricken.

"This is where I cut you off, both lit'rally and figuratively." He raised the hatchet over his head and was ready to swing down when Madison screamed, "Okay! Okay! Wait!"

"Okay – what?"

"I'll give it to you. Fine."

"I thought you said it was in the briefcase."

Madison reached down into a place that is prohibited in public by law and produced the thumb drive. "Here."

Harper was hesitant to take it from her. "Do you have a rag or something?"

"What? Are you joking?"

"Well, first you lie to me about where it is, and then you pull it out of – well – *there!* And, yeah, all of this after you spit on me. Now wipe that thing off before I go ahead and finish what I was getting ready to do with this hatchet, ya dumb sea cow."

Begrudgingly, Tara Madison wiped the thumb drive off and handed it over to Harper.

"That wasn't too hard, was it?"

"I hope you're happy."

"My therapist tells me the same thing."

And in that moment, while they were ducking for cover and

more bodies were falling, Black Ice and Harper, well, they just never connected.

"I guess you think you did me a favor pinning me down."

"I pretty much saved your life." Harper agreed. "Believe me, my friends are shooting from – like – other atmospheres, and they're lucky if they can hit a blimp, bad as they are."

"Kill her, Harper," Kinley's voice came through the com.

Harper pulled his last gun and held it tight to Madison's head.

"Kill me," she said. "I'd do the same to you."

"Killing you would be doing you a favor, and I'm just not in the favor-doing business. Not tonight, at least."

"You leave me alive, and I swear to God that I will find you and kill you."

"Aww, now you shouldn't swear to God. I'm pretty sure He's not a big fan of people doing that," Harper smiled.

"Kill her, for the love of Pete!" Kinley repeated his order.

"See ya 'round downtown, Ice." Harper fired his weapon.

"She dead?" Kinley asked.

"As good as – besides I got what we came for." And from there Harper Rowe got up, ran to the nearest ledge and jumped. He enjoyed the freefall for about two seconds, then he pulled the ripcord on his fanny pack which turned into a base jumping parachute.

Harper held the thumb drive tightly in his left hand as he drifted peacefully off the top of the east Polanco tower and descended through the humid night air. Unfortunately, a sudden brisk wind picked up and drove him into the side wall of an opposing building. From there, he free fell some twenty feet to the asphalt.

"Ouch," he said, wincing. "If you guys are still out there – come pick me up. I have just landed somewhere between here and eternity."

"I'm off the roof and tracking your cell phone beacon," Chase said.

"Me, too, Harp. Hang in there, man."

"I think I punctured a lung," Harper said as he rolled around on the pavement of one of Mexico City's back alleys. "I got the thumb drive, although at this point, it may be permanently impaled into my abdomen."

Harper lay there for a moment and then he said, "Kinley, I see the bright lights of Heaven's gates. I think I'm going home."

"It's just me, ya stupid idiot," Chase said as she got out of the van. "You're seeing the lights of my van." She rushed to Harper and picked him up with both of her arms, carried him to the van, and with two fingers opened the side door. "This is going to hurt," she said as she tossed him into the back of the van. "Sorry."

"You have the bedside manner of Genghis Khan."

"I said, 'Sorry.' I'm not your mother."

Chase slammed the door shut, ran around to the driver's side and hopped up behind the steering wheel. She was just about to put the pedal down when the passenger side door opened.

"Room for one more?" Devereaux asked as he showed up from nowhere.

"Get in. We gotta go."

Devereaux got in and shut the door tight behind him. "I heard you say that you were tracking the beacon on Harper's cell phone so I did the same. Speaking of that, I think now would be a good time for all of us to get rid of our cells. If we can track them then there's no telling who else can."

Chase rolled down her window and chucked her phone. Devereaux handed his to her to do the same.

Rowe groaned as he retrieved his own phone and tossed it up to Kinley who, in turn, handed it to Laurie to dispose of as well.

"Where are we going?" Kin asked.

"Anywhere but here," Laurie said.

"I have a place for us to go. While you were up on your rooftop sharpening your nails, I was making a few calls. I got us a flight outta here, but we have to be there soon. Go to the airstrip where you picked us up."

"Really? I don't have fond memories of that place."

"Go already, will ya. Time to make some positive memories at that place.

Laurie Chase tromped down on the accelerator and headed for the airstrip.

Kinley crawled into the back of the van and slid next to Harper. He took his head into his hands. "How ya feelin', man?"

"Like a used diaper."

"Wow. I think I just threw up in my mouth."

"I feel like that, too."

"Tell him to hang on," Chase said as she drove into the night.

"We're gonna get you better, boss. Just hang on," Devereaux urged.

"So why aren't we going back to the house?" Agent Chase asked.

"Well, you can call me a negative Nancy, but I feel quite confident that Secretary Michaels has most likely sent some guys like me and Harper to take care of me and Harper – and you, as well. They're probably sitting right outside of the house now just waiting for us to return. The dude has killed so many people over this stupid thumb drive, there's no reason to feel like we're exempt from his madness, too. When we get to the airfield, the plane will have a computer on board. I cannot wait to see what is on this thing."

"All my stuff is at the house. Clothes – jewelry – books –everything."

"Well, now you can update that wardrobe of yours. Maybe at some point you can come back here. I don't know. I just don't know."

"So, we get on that plane and then what? I mean, where are we going, and what are we going to do once we get there?"

"We're flying back to D.C. where I hope we can get this mess behind us."

"And how do you think we are going to do that?"

"We're going to give the thumb drive to Secretary Michaels. Maybe then he'll stop killing people, and maybe we can trade the drive for him to forget about us. From there – I don't know about you – but I'm going to disappear, spend the rest of my days in anonymity and hope that I don't grow old too soon from having to look over my shoulder every day wondering if someone's got a bullet waiting for me."

Harper spoke up, "Can we stop at a pharmacy or something? Get some aspirins and one of those heat wraps."

"Yeah, buddy. Just tell us what ya need."

"Something. Anything. Just get me something fast. As best as I can tell, I have three broken ribs, two of the fingers on my left hand are dislocated, pretty sure my left shoulder is separated, and I can't seem to wiggle my toes."

"Geez, Harp. How are you not screaming in agony?"

"I'm just too tired to scream at this point."

"Here," Devereaux said suddenly, "on the right. Pharmacy." He looked down at his ailing friend. "Hang in there, Harper. We're gonna get ya fixed up as best we can, and then we're going home."

"Make no mistake about it, Kin. We may be going back to the states, but I'm pretty sure we won't be going home. Not back to your 18th floor apartment, and not back to my new White Marsh town house."

"I'll go in," said Laurie. My money's already switched over to the local currency anyway. What do I need to get?"

"Gauze, tape, bandages, pain killers, cold compresses, heat packs. The dude needs a hospital, but the only hospital he's going to get is me and you and whatever you can grab in there."

"Back in a flash, then." And Laurie Chase was out of the van and into the pharmacy.

"She gone?" Harper asked.

"She'll be back in a few. Just hang in there, man. We're gonna get ya fixed up as best we can," Devereaux reassured.

"Good," Rowe said as he pulled the com out of his ear and stuck it in his pocket. He looked at his friend with an expression that told him to do the same.

Once Kinley had repeated his partner's action, Harper said, "Now that she's gone – I'm fine." Rowe began coughing hard. He spit some phlegm out onto the van floor. "Okay, maybe I'm not *fine*, but I will be. You got a plane flying us back to the states, for real?"

"Yeah, it's going to take us to a small landing field just north of D.C."

"Great," Harper said through pained breaths. "Once we get there, you and Chase go wherever you need to go. You've got enough papers and money there for the two of you to disappear. Do it. This whole thing is my fault – I'm the one that went up those stairs when you told me not to – and I'm the one that needs to stay behind and take the heat."

"No way, kid. Forget that."

"Kinley, I'm in no shape to argue. Without you and her, I would've never made it this far, but I have – *we* have. I've got the thumb drive so, like you said, maybe I can use it to bargain for our lives back. If I can't, I'll just be happy to know that you and Chase are on a planet far, far away by then."

Devereaux was silent, and his face had a pensive look on it.

"Come on, Kin, if you don't want to do it for you then, at least, do it for her. I mean, sure, you did make the conscious choice to come along with me on this wild ride, but she sure didn't. In the last few days her life has been turned around more times than a Rubik's cube at a dunce convention. She never wanted to be any part of this. Take her somewhere so that she can get some semblance of an existence back, okay?"

"Okay, I'll think about it. I'll think about it once we see

what's on that thumb drive, and I'll think about it once we see just how *fine* you really are. Until then, it's the three of us seeing this thing through."

Harper wanted to reply, but before he could, Laurie opened the side door to the van and dropped two big plastic bags full of medical supplies at Kinley's feet. "How's he doing?" she asked.

"Get us to that airstrip. I'll have a much better prognosis at that point."

She got ready to shut the door but then asked, "Hey, did you guys turn off your coms?"

"Yeah," Kin lied. "We're all together now. No need for them anymore."

An understanding look came across Laurie's face. "Yeah. Good point." She slammed the side door of the van, got back behind the wheel, pulled out of the pharmacy parking lot and sped toward the airstrip.

Headed Home

When Secretary of Defense Paul Michaels's phone rang, he was expecting it to be DEA Agent Laurie Chase calling to let him know the outcome of the night's operation to retrieve the stolen thumb drive. He had been awaiting her call for some time now. So when it was Agent Jeb Crool on the other end, he was very disappointed. He was even more disappointed with what Crool had to report.

"Sir, they have not shown up here yet. You gave me the DEA agent's cell phone number so I took the liberty of triangulating her position. She was in the vicinity of the Polanco Twin Towers for a while, but then she went on the move. For the last twenty minutes the signal has been at a standstill. We've been listening to a local scanner, and there's a ton of action over there so something has obviously gone down like you thought. How long do you want us to sit on this house, sir?"

Michaels began to fume. He was sure that he had Laurie Chase right in the palm of his hand and that he could count on her. He had taken major steps to ensure this, and now that it appeared that she had crossed him, he was angry beyond words.

He thought about what to do. As a precautionary measure, he had already sent men to all the major airports to ensure that she and

Kinley Devereaux and Harper Rowe could not try to make a last minute attempt to escape the situation by trying to leave the country in a hurry.

"Sir?" Crool asked.

"Leave one of your men there to sit on the house. I'm going to issue a BOLO to every airport, border crossing, international point of travel, and to our Mexican embassy to be sure that they don't try to hole up in some other local flophouse, safe house, or outhouse that we control down there. We *will* find them in the next two hours."

"I'll leave one of my guys here," Crool agreed, "but where do you want us to go?"

"There's a private U.S.-controlled airstrip that they might try to use. They flew in on it this morning. They may somehow try to use it to get out of there. I'll send you the coordinates to get to it. If I hear anything as to where they might be, I will let you know immediately."

"Roger that, sir. I'll be awaiting those coordinates, and we will be there forthwith."

Paul Michaels slammed down the phone and stood up and grabbed the chair he had been sitting in and threw it against his office wall, swearing all the while.

The person that Kinley had contacted while he was up on top of the Zircon Building was named Genoveva Werner. She was a German national that Kinley had worked with several times on jobs in Berlin, Rio de Janeiro, Seattle, and other places. Genoveva was in the transport business and had helped Kinley out of several tight spots when he needed last minute travel to depart or get into places where he was doing jobs. She was one of several contacts that he had called earlier in the evening. It so happened that Genoveva was just coming off of a job and was on a golf trip in Scottsdale, Arizona. Getting to the private airfield that was just outside of Mexico City on short notice would not be a problem for her.

Twenty minutes after fleeing the parking lot of the drug store, Laurie Chase wielded the van wildly through the gate of the airstrip. The debris from that morning's shootout was still strewn about the premises.

"Geez," Chase said in astonishment, "that's not a small plane. That's a small jet!"

"Of course. First class in, first class out."

The aircraft that Chase was looking at was a seven passenger Mitsubishi MU-300 Diamond IA jet.

Chase pulled right up to it, jumped out of the van and ran around to the side door to help Kinley with Harper. As she did, she heard that the jet's engines were already running. The side door of the van began to open. "So, now that we're here, how is he?"

"I got him patched up as best as I could. His left shoulder was out of joint, so I had to pop that back in. He ain't much to look at, but I think he'll survive. Here, grab his arm."

Harper slid his feet out of the van and onto the ground. He put his right arm around Chase and she pulled him up. Kinley was out right behind him and gingerly put Harper's left arm around his shoulder. They slowly and carefully walked him over to the steps of the IA. At the top of the staircase the silhouette of a tall, thin German woman filled the entrance to the craft.

"*Heilige scheisse*, is he okay?" Genoveva asked in horror.

"He'll be fine once we get him up these stairs. No need for watching this circus, love. We got 'im. Get in that cockpit and get ready for takeoff. I'll be up to give you the go-ahead in just a few."

Werner took Kinley's suggestion and moved expeditiously back to the jet's cockpit, strapped in, and readied things for an immediate departure. Within the minute Devereaux was yelling from the back, "We're in, Gen. Pull up those stairs and let's go, baby!"

Jeb Crool had been driving like a maniac to get to the airstrip, but as he neared his destination, he realized his best efforts had not been enough. He slammed his hands in disgust against the steering wheel while he watched the Diamond IA fly off into the black Mexican sky. He wasted no time in contacting Secretary Michaels. "Sir, you were right. They came to the airstrip. My men and I got here too late. I'm watching them go now. I'm terribly sorry, Mr. Secretary."

"Get to the airport and get back here as soon as you can, Agent Crool," the Secretary of Defense instructed. He hung up in anger.

Crool put his cell on the dashboard.

"What did he say?" asked the agent that was sitting in the front passenger seat.

"We're headed home."

Jeb U-turned the rental car and headed back into the city. He smiled slightly. For as little as he knew about what was going on, he was glad he did not have to pull the trigger on anyone tonight. While he was disappointed in the wasted time on a wasted mission, his conscience certainly felt better.

"I can't thank you enough," said a relieved Kinley Devereaux as he took a seat in the copilot's chair. "I'm going to need you to stay low and off the radar as much as you can on this flight."

"Are we being targeted?" Werner inquired.

"Not sure, really, but after everything that we've been through, I'd just as soon not take any chances."

"I've already called ahead. We've got an unofficial flight plan – meaning that we have a flight plan, but unless it becomes absolutely necessary it's completely off the books until we land – and at this time of night and for where we're going, that shouldn't be a problem. I'm going to take us on a direct line out over the ocean, and then we will circle back around into our destination so that we don't have to fly over any U.S. airspace until we come in from off the coast. After we do hit U.S. airspace, we'll be landing in about fifteen minutes so it will be quick. I'll drop you and your two friends and be gone before we're even a blip on anyone's radar. Should be on the ground in about three hours and fifteen minutes, give or take. I'll bill you through regular channels?"

"Yes, definitely. You know the routine."

"Just so ya know, this will be double time. I was on vacation after all," she smiled.

"For the mess you just pulled us out of, I'll pay you double time and throw in a set of steak knives. Hey, not to change the subject—"

"Yes," Genoveva cut him off, "there's a laptop in the overhead compartment right behind where you're sitting. It's fully charged so you needn't worry about a power source. Just turn it on and go."

"Thank you," Devereaux said as he got up and retrieved the laptop. He grabbed Genoveva's shoulder and gave it a squeeze and repeated his gratitude, "Thank you."

The Mystery of the Thumb Drive Revealed

When Kinley came back into the cabin of the jet, he found his bandaged-up partner fully reclined in his seat and fast asleep. Seated across from Harper, Laurie Chase was also in a completely reclined position and dead to the world.

"Harper," Devereaux said in a hushed tone as he ever so gently nudged his friend. "Harper, give me that thumb drive."

Rowe opened his eyes and groggily looked at Kin. "What?"

"The thumb drive. It's time to find out just what it is that we've been risking our lives for over the last day and a half."

Harper winced in pain as he dug the thumb drive out and handed it to Kinley, who was now in the seat next to him. Devereaux put the drive into the laptop and punched a few keys.

"Here we go."

A set of blueprints came onto the laptop's screen. And then another. And then another.

And then another. Kin was quick to diminish them down until he got back to the original screen. He and Harper looked thoroughly at the layout.

"Pull up some of those other ones," Harper suggested.

Kinley did. The two men studied each one just as comprehensively as the previous one as they tried to mentally link them together. Kin pulled up a third set of prints, and the duo pored over these for a few minutes before Harper commented, "They all look like different angles of the same thing."

"Yeah, and I think I can tell what this *thing* is, but I just – I just can't believe that it's real. What do you think it is?"

"A space shuttle. An extremely unrealistically high-tech space shuttle."

Devereaux looked at his partner. "That's what I'm seeing, too." Once again he diminished all the screens back to the original. "Like this right here," he pointed to the monitor. "It's not just a unique design – if this is real – it's completely groundbreaking."

"Hey, Laurie," Rowe called out to the sleeping woman.

She opened her eyes and abruptly lifted her head. "What? Are we there?"

"No," answered Devereaux. "We just want you to come over here and look at this. We stuck the drive into this laptop, and you really need to see this. Confirm that what we're seeing here is really what we're seeing here."

Begrudgingly, the DEA agent put her seat into the upright position, stood up and moved over toward the two men. Devereaux moved down a seat so that Laurie could sit between him and Harper. Once she was seated, he put the computer on her lap.

Having just come out of a deep sleep, Chase was having a hard time focusing her eyes on the screen. She opened them wide and then squinted in an attempt to clear her vision. After repeating this sequence several times the image on the computer became more defined. "You're looking at one set of blueprints. There are three other ones down there," Devereaux explained as he pointed to the bottom of the screen.

Laurie took some time to look at the first set of blueprints before she progressed to the second set and then the third and then the fourth. She shuffled back and forth between the four simulacrums for several minutes. Harp and Kin were patient while she soaked it all in.

"This can't be for real," she finally said.

"Kinda what we thought, too," Rowe said.

"But then when you take into consideration how many people have been killed in the last 36 hours because of what we're looking at, it tends to lend a bit of legitimacy to it," Kinley followed up.

Chase looked at Devereaux on her left and at Rowe on her right, then back to the laptop screen. "It's just not possible," she paused, "is it?"

"If this is real, we're looking at technological breakthrough that will allow this particular space shuttle to take off and land with the ease and preparation that it takes for your average person to pull in and out of their driveway."

"And that's just the launching and landing. With what I see here, once this craft is actually *in* outer space – this could change the course of the entire human race. Whatever nation has this technology first would certainly have the upper hand to world domination for awhile. I can see why Secretary Michaels was so hellbent on getting it back."

"So – what you're saying is – it's possible?" Chase asked nervously.

"Just from the short, harried, and distracted glance I got of the people on that rooftop tonight, I'd say there were people from 20 to 30 countries. That would be a significant number of nations to be represented for something that was just conjecture and speculation. A lot of people have died in the last day and a half over what we have here. Once confirmed, countries will go to war for technology like this."

"So, what do we do with it?" asked Laurie.

"We're in no frame of mind to be making a decision about

something like this," Kinley said. "We're all tired and fritzed out of our minds. I've made a call to a guy that I know that is about as far off the grid as you can get. Once we land, he's going to pick us up and take us some place that will be safe for a few hours. We'll go there, get some much-needed rest, and when we wake up with refreshed and clear minds, then we can make a plan about this."

"I'm down with that," Harper acquiesced. "I am way too tired to think clearly at this point. Shoot, I was in so much pain just a couple of hours ago – now I'm just too tired to even feel any of *that* much less feel some obligatory notion of right or wrong."

"And I'm too tired to disagree with either of you," Chase said.

Landing, Sleeping, and Waking

Genoveva was completely accurate with her assessment of the flight, the landing, and her departure. The flight was three hours and twenty minutes and the landing consisted of her three clients deplaning, her giving Devereaux a friendly hug goodbye, and her taking back off again about ten minutes later.

Devereaux's friend Rob Perry was there to pick them up. Once in his car and on their way, Devereaux asked, "You got someplace safe for us to sack out, right?"

"No worries, chief. I got a bar that the government doesn't even know about. Over top of that undisclosed bar I have a nice unused two-bedroom apartment. It's got a regular exit, an emergency exit, and an 'Oh crap, the emergency exit is no good' exit. It's cool, though, you won't even have to worry about the last two exits. This place is so secluded, I'm pretty sure the three of ya's could walk out of there buck naked with sparklers coming out of your fannies, and no one would even notice. You guys will be fine."

"How long till we get there?"

Ten seconds later Perry stopped the car and said, "We're here." He pointed out the passenger side window, "You're there." Devereaux, Rowe, and Chase looked to their right to see a quaint looking little bar.

"Happy campin', troopers," Rob said as the trio got out of the car.

They walked into the bar, which was pretty dead, even for a Sunday afternoon. The bartender saw the three of them. "Devereaux? Party of three?" he asked non-specifically.

"Yeah, that's us," Kin answered.

"Through that door, take a right and up the stairs."

"Thanks." The trio did as instructed and found themselves in a nice two-bedroom apartment.

"Who wants to sleep where?" Harper asked tiredly.

"You're with me," Chase said as she grabbed Devereaux's arm and dragged him into one of the bedrooms.

Harper went into the other bedroom and flopped down on its bed. He did not know how long he was asleep before his friend came in and woke him up.

"Dev, you're here," he said groggily.

"Chase is out cold. We need to figure out what we're gonna do about this."

"What do you want to do?"

"Seeing what we've seen, and knowing what we think we know – this is obviously a lot bigger than all of us."

"Yeah, it is. That's why I still like my initial plan of the two of you getting yourselves out of Dodge as soon as you can. If the three of us try to ride this out, we're all going to get killed. You and Chase get out of here. I'll use the thumb drive to buy you guys some time, and then I'll try to exchange the drive with Secretary Michaels in exchange for his leaving me alone. Maybe I'll come join the two of you on whatever island you decide to escape to."

"Ya can't give him the thumb drive, Harp. Ya can't give it to anyone. You know that, right? The implications will be global."

"Hey, man. I get what you're saying. I do, but technology is technology. We may be able to postpone the inevitable by destroying this drive, but that's just for now. Whoever thought of this is out there somewhere, and he or she can duplicate it at some point. If what is on this thumb drive is legit then it's going to come to fruition eventually. You and Chase get someplace safe, and I'm going to do what I have to do."

Devereaux handed the thumb drive to his friend. "Do you have any freakin' clue what you're going to do?"

"Yeah, I have a good idea," and Harper got up off the bed and hugged his friend.

"I thought when you went up on that roof in Mexico City you were sacrificing yourself for the team, but what you're doing now," and Kinley got a little choked up, "this is probably gonna get you killed for real. Secretary Michaels is just one of the worries. Once word gets out about what's on that drive – I can't imagine how many people are going to be gunning for it."

Harper broke the embrace. "I've never minded dying for what I believed in."

"So what are you gonna do?"

"What do you think I'm gonna do?"

"I think you're going to do what you think is right – and kill everybody that gets in your way in the process."

"Yeah, that sounds about right," Harper smiled.

"You take care of yourself, man," Kinley said as he wiped a tear from his cheek. "I love ya, kid."

"I know," Harper said as he patted Kin's shoulder. "You take care of you – and her."

"Be safe," Devereaux said.

And as he walked away and down the stairs from the two-bedroom apartment, Harper hollered, "See ya 'round downtown, Kinley."

Two Days Later

Secretary of Defense Paul Michaels returned to his office after attending a press conference at which he vowed the United States' full support of Mexico after the terrorist acts that had transpired in Mexico City over the weekend. He had just sat back down at his desk when Linda Powell came across his phone intercom, "Sir, I have a call on line one from a Harper Rowe. He said he needed to speak with you immediately. Do you want to take this call, Mr. Secretary?"

Paul Michaels had been using every favor owed to him to track down Laurie Chase, Kinley Devereaux, and Harper Rowe over the last forty-eight hours – all to absolutely no avail. He was almost to the point of giving up, but now one of them was calling him. For a moment he hesitated.

"Sir, I can take a message, if you'd like," Linda said.

"No, no, Linda. You can put him through."

Silence – and then a click.

"Mr. Secretary?"

"Mr. Rowe?"

"Yeah, you bet it's *Mr. Rowe*. Don't talk, just listen." Harper was silent for a moment to make sure the Secretary of Defense was indeed listening. "I just saw your press conference," he began again, "and I have to figure that they haven't identified all the bodies from that rooftop in Mexico City just yet because if they had they would've found the remains of one U.S. DEA Agent Laurie Chase and one Mr. Kinley Devereaux – both Americans. In which case you would have known that this was not a terrorist attack, but instead, a move which was made by Americans. Unless, of course, you already did know this and in that press conference you were lying your cheeks off to the United States as a whole. But I'm willing to give you the benefit of the doubt on this one."

"What do you want, Mr. Rowe?"

Harper laughed. "It's not what I want, Mr. Secretary. It's what you want. My cohorts and I went up on that rooftop, under your command, to get something that was stolen from your Under Secretary's house a few nights ago – a thumb drive with top secret documents on it. And while I lost a couple friends in the process, I was able to procure said thumb drive, and now I want to exchange it with you."

"Why would I ever believe you, Mr. Rowe. Why would I even begin to give in to such a silly notion that you have that thumb drive."

"Because if you don't, I just might be on the next flight out on that space shuttle that you want so badly to be built."

Harper was silent.

Secretary Michaels was silent.

"Listening now, aren't ya, jerk wad?"

"Yes, I'm listening. What are your demands?"

"My demands are pretty simple, Mr. Secretary. I'll give you the thumb drive in exchange for your promise to leave me alone the rest of my days. And if ya don't, I'll blow the whistle on this whole charade."

"And just how, pray tell, will you do that, Mr. Rowe?"

"The conversations you had with DEA Agent Chase while she was in Mexico City should be enough, but if they aren't, I do have copies of the blueprints that were on the thumb drive. The two of them combined should be enough to cut you off at the nads, Mr. Secretary."

"Now I know you're lying. That drive was made so that it could not possibly be copied in any possible way. Nice try, Mr. Rowe."

"Now I know you're a complete stooge, Secretary Michaels. It never occurred to me to try to copy the drive. I just took pictures of the computer screen while I was looking at the blueprints. You'll forgive me if I'm so much of a lo-tech guy that I used a Polaroid."

Michaels was stymied. "So, we meet and you give me the drive. What about the recordings and the photos?"

"Those are my life insurance policies. They'll never be on me so even if you find me and kill me, they will be with someone else that knows what to do with them and how to do it. You wanted my demands, well, there they are. We meet in two hours in front of the Lincoln Memorial – you *will* come alone – and if I see anyone around there that doesn't look like you, then I'm gone. We are clear on this, yes?"

"We're clear," Michaels said.

"Good. Don't make this difficult then. Show up, I'll give you the drive, I walk away, and we both go back to our regularly scheduled lives already in progress."

"Just so I have it straight – I'll see you at 4:30 in front of the Lincoln Memorial?"

But Harper was gone.

SHOWDOWN

Michaels did as he was told and made his way to the Lincoln Memorial.

And he came alone.

And he had directed five different marksmen to shoot Harper Rowe once he had given up the thumb drive. The snipers were placed at 1:00, 4:00, 6:00, 8:00, and 10:00 positions around the pre-arranged rendezvous point. All ready to fire.

Harper was brave enough to show up. Scared to death, he stood in front of the Lincoln Memorial and awaited the arrival of Secretary of Defense Paul Michaels.

He did not look around, for he was afraid of what he might see. He knew that today he was on his own.

Instead of looking around, he pulled out his phone and started playing Tetris on it. He was well into his game when he heard the booming voice of Paul Michaels.

"Mr. Rowe!"

"Hang on, Mr. Secretary." Harper busily punched a few more keys on his phone and then looked up. "Yeah! Level 77 on Tetris – sir."

"Are you quite finished with your phone games?"

Harper pushed a few more buttons and then put his phone away. "I saved the game, so, yeah – for now."

"The thumb drive – and then you can get back to your game."

"No need to be pushy, Mr. Secretary. Obviously you have anywhere from one to a hundred guns aimed at my head. Despite my blackmail attempts, you are foolhardy enough in your ways to believe that you can thwart my threats against you. Nothing wrong with that at all. Still, I believe that my people are better than yours, so I will give you the thumb drive in my foolhardy way, knowing that in my death – I will bury you."

"So, do you know what you have?"

"I do not."

"The safety of the human race."

"Wow. That's awesome."

"It's a prototype, Mr. Rowe."

"For what?"

"To stop the end of the world."

"Maybe to stop the end of *your* world. Good golly, man," Harper continued, "don't you realize what this is? It's an opportunity to get to know realms way, way, way beyond our dreams. You want to use this as a means to defend what we know when it could be something that could be used to develop things way beyond our capacity of thinking. I believe in God. I believe in a Heaven and a hell, but if there is something more to be known – I want to know about it. What is on this drive is our way of getting to explore that."

"So, you do know what you have," said Secretary Michaels.

"It's a space shuttle that can go up and come down with the regularity of a helicopter."

"The current administration could not give a crap about our space race. Our President has made NASA nothing more than window dressing. Our space program made us a nation. You do know that, don't you, Mr. Rowe?" Secretary Michaels pleaded. "I could sure use a man like you. Are you positive you don't want to come to work for me?"

"I'd rather work for an electric toothbrush salesman in Amish country."

"Just give me the drive, Mr. Rowe."

"You blame the current administration. Hey, you're right. The current administration hasn't made us a bunch of killers like you, Mr. Secretary. It's just made us lazy. A bunch of blamers. It's never our fault. We're a product of the system."

"Give it, Mr. Rowe."

"Fine. It's your death warrant."

Harper dug deep into his underwear, pulled out the drive, and presented it to Secretary of Defense Paul Michaels. As he held it up in presentation, a gunshot went off.

A bullet went right through the thumb drive and into the heart of Paul Michaels.

"Oh, crap stew!" Rowe said and hit the ground in a panic. He found some safety behind the nearest thing he could get to – a park bench. Several joggers in the area scattered in a frenzy as well, and one of them took cover behind the same park bench. She landed on top of him.

"Sorry," she said as she rolled off of him and ducked for cover.

Harper was quick to jump on her to protect her as another handful of gunshots rang out. "It's okay. I got you."

She was so frightened that she let him. The two of them lay together for a minute or so.

Harper was the first to realize that the danger had passed. He pulled back off the woman.

"I think we're okay," he said. The woman slowly lifted her head.

She was beautiful. Her intense green eyes contrasted with her porcelain white skin. She reached up and pulled her long chestnut brown hair out of her face. She looked at Harper in total awe.

"You just saved my life," she said.

"Yeah, I probably did."

"I don't even know you – and you were just willing sacrifice yourself for me."

"Are you okay? Are you hurt?"

"How do I thank you for something like that? Seriously?"

"I'm Harper Rowe."

"I'm Wendy."

"Hi, Wendy," Harper said shaking her hand. "Do you live around here?"

Contact

Harper stayed with Wendy in the following week, using her computer to try to reach out to Kinley.

He was scared to death. He wondered if the people that had killed Secretary Michaels were going to come gunning for him next. But at this point he had run out of ideas for how to contact Kinley.

Harper was ready to cut ties with reality and run away with Wendy in a way only he knew how. And that's when he heard from his friend.

By email. In one of his thirteen email accounts.

It read:

> **Lost Souls Restaurant. Day after tomorrow.**
> **See you then.**
>
> **Fudd Duck**

Ending

Harper approached the Lost Souls Restaurant's entrance with complete caution. He discreetly looked up and down the streets and sidewalks to make sure there were no signs of surveillance or imminent danger. Satisfied with what he did and did not see, he entered the restaurant.

A maître d' walked up to him immediately. "Good afternoon, sir. Just one?

"No. I'm here to meet someone."

"Oh? Is your party here already?"

Harper looked around until he saw Kinley Devereaux sitting in a booth in the back corner. "Yup, sure is." Harper walked right past the maître d' and navigated his way back to the booth where his friend was.

Upon seeing Harper approaching, Kinley stood up to greet his friend. He extended his hand to shake Harper's. "Good to see ya, man."

"Wasn't sure if you were gonna show, Kin."

"Why? Why wouldn't I show?"

"I'm a little worried these days since we parted ways. Still, I know that I can always count on you."

"I asked you to meet me here, Harp. Why wouldn't I be here?"

"Not sure if you've seen the news, but they assassinated the Secretary of Defense. I can't help but think that they – whoever *they* might be – will be coming after you and me next."

Eh, I don't worry about that. I needed you to come here so we could say a proper goodbye like friends do. I think you know that, at this point, we need to go our separate ways."

"Yeah, I know, Kin. I do know this."

"Hey, I want you to do something for me." Kinley reached inside of his jacket and pulled out a cell phone and slid it across the table to his friend. "I need you to keep that cell phone on you at all times. Never let it out of your sight. Okay?"

"Okay. Why?"

"Ya just never know when we might need each other, Harper. I'll call you one of these days. I will. I promise."

"But when?"

"I don't know. It might be next week. It might be next year. It might be next decade. Honest to Pete – I don't know when, but it sure would make me feel safe and secure to know that if I needed to call you that I could. So, if you don't mind, just keep that on you and within your eyesight at all times."

"And if I need to call you?"

"I'll be on the other end. You've got my promise."

"I guess I can deal with that." Rowe put the phone in his jacket pocket. "Hear anything from Chase?"

"No, man, she's gone with the wind."

"That's too bad. I really thought the two of you had a thing."

Devereaux looked at his friend incredulously. "You're kidding, right?"

"No. I mean – I thought – she and I had nothing. I thought the two of you were getting on just fine. No?"

"No."

"Well, what about Kelly? Any word from her? Any word *about* her?"

"Nothing," he sighed as he ran his hand over his mouth and stroked his beard, "and it hasn't been for a lack of trying either." Kinley took a drink from the glass of water that was sitting on the table, and then he said, "One last thing, Harper. That thing you told me about a couple weeks ago before any of this even started – that story about the faithful man – I get it now. I have found my faith now."

"In the right things?"

"Yes, definitely in the right things, my brother."

Harper smiled a relieved smile. "That makes me smile, but I do need to ask you this. As far as the life here on earth is concerned, I really feel like whoever it was that shot the SOD is going to come gunning for me and you next."

"Is that what you think? That whomever it was that shot the Secretary of Defense is going to shoot you next?"

"Yes. That is exactly what I think."

Devereaux stood up from his seat at the table, looked down at his seated partner and said, "Relax, Harp. I'm not going to shoot you."

With that, Kinley made his way from around the table and toward the door. He reached down and patted his friend on the back. "See ya 'round downtown, Harp," and walked out the door of the Lost Souls Restaurant.

Harper sat in stunned silence.

By the time he came to his senses, he stood up and went after his friend for some answers. He walked out of the Lost Souls Restaurant and looked up and down the sidewalk and back and forth across the street.

Devereaux was gone.

Harper missed his friend already. But he knew he had some things that needed tending. He returned to where he and Devereaux had been sitting, left a gratuity on the table, and went out on his own to take care of a few loose ends.

A WORD FROM DOC

Thank you for reading *Chasing Black Ice*.
I hope you enjoyed it.

Please read on, because I've included an excerpt
of the trio's continuing story in *Chasing Revenge*,
book two of the Boom!!...Killers. series.

I occasionally send newsletters with details on
new releases, special offers, and other bits of
news relating to my characters. If you would like
to sign up to the mailing list, please go to:

www.goldenalleypress.com/boom-killers-series

You can make a difference . . .

Reviews are the most powerful weapon I have
when it comes to getting my books noticed.
Honest reviews help bring them to the attention
of other readers.

If you've enjoyed this book, please consider
leaving a review on Amazon.com. You can
jump right to the page by using this link:
www.tinyurl.com/review-chasing-black-ice

Doc

If you enjoyed *Chasing Black Ice*,
please keep reading for an exciting preview of

CHASING REVENGE

Boom!!...Killers.
SERIES BOOK #2

Doc Ephraim Bates

Available in print and ebook from
Golden Alley Press

AWKWARD

"David," she poked him. It was around 3:30 a.m.

He was a light sleeper and woke up amazingly aware and attentive.

"Can I ask you a question?" she asked.

"Can it wait till morning?" David whispered.

"We've been dating for almost three months," she continued, disregarding his request, "and I know you've told me that the second cell phone that you keep with you at all times is nothing more than a memento of a friend that you used to have, but..." She stopped awkwardly for a moment.

"But?"

"Just not sure how comfortable I am with you having that."

David Pleasance scooched himself up in the bed that he and his girlfriend, Michelle Runkle, shared. "What?"

"Yeah, it makes me feel uncomfortable."

"My cell phone that I never use?"

"Yeah."

"I've let you check it at your leisure whenever you wanted to in the last few weeks. I'm not using it for anything. Just something that I keep on me. Kinda like that locket that you keep around your neck that reminds you of your mom."

"Yeah, I know, but..." She went silent.

"But?" David asked again.

"But other guys can't call me on my mother's locket."

"Michelle, I feel pretty confident that other guys aren't going to call me, either."

"It's just weird, is all."

"It's three-thirty in the morning, and you want to talk to me about a cell phone that I never get calls on. That's pretty stinkin' weird, too." Pleasance rolled over and away from her and pulled the covers up over his shoulder. "Get some sleep, baby. Tomorrow's a new day."

The couple stopped arguing and began to resume their slumber.

Pleasance had his back to Michelle. She reluctantly moved in behind him, assumed the spoon position, and fell asleep with her arms around him.

It may have been fifteen minutes, but then again, it could have been a few hours. She heard it first.

"David, your phone's ringing," she mumbled, half awake.

Pleasance heard it and answered it quickly. It was not his regular cell that was ringing – it was his second cell phone. The cell phone that just moments – or hours – ago Michelle had been making a fuss about. The cell phone that he said he never gets calls on.

He answered it so it would stop ringing, so Michelle would not have time to notice the difference between his regular cell phone ring and this odd new ring. To his credit, he had tried to set his second cell ringtone to one that was similar to his usual ringtone. And although it had been a long time since it last rang, he immediately recognized the difference.

Pleasance stealthily crawled out of bed.

"Kin?" he asked in a hushed yet excited whisper.

"I can assure you it's not Mother Theresa, David Pleasance."

"Yeah," Harper said. "I'm pretty sure she's dead."

I Need a Favor

"You able to talk?" Devereaux asked.

"Yeah, just give me a second," Harper said in a susurrated tone as he hurriedly made his way out of the bedroom, down the hall, and into the kitchen. "I'm good now."

"David Pleasance." Kinley said dryly. "Hmm, that has a nice peaceful, serene sound to it. So, what number alias is this one?"

"I don't know. I seem to change up identities about once every two to three weeks. Bounce around amongst seven or eight different ones. By the way, how did you know I was going by David Pleasance these days?"

"Same way I know that Michelle Runkle is your current housemate. I keep tabs on you as much as I can."

"It's been eighteen months – give or take – since Mexico City. You've been spyin' on me for that long?"

"Not spying, just keeping tabs. In a way, you could say that I have been your guardian angel – only slightly more violent than your standard guardian angel. But, yeah, you definitely ain't kiddin' about moving around a lot. I've seen nomads trying to avoid a bench warrant that didn't move around as much as you do."

"Yeah, well, I guess it's a little bit easier for you, buddy. Everyone thinks you died up on that rooftop in Mexico City. I've still got people trying to track me down, and the majority of them coming from your United States Government."

"Hey, if you keep showing your face then they're going to know where you are."

"Make no mistake about it, Kin. I show my face not so that they will know where I am, but rather so I will know where they are."

"Oh, is that what your strategy is?"

"Precisely."

"That worries me."

"What? My strategy?"

"No. The fact that I agree with your technique. By the way, nice job on tidying up those last few loose ends from the situation in Mexico City. You saved me from having to take care of it."

"Think nothing of it," Harper tiptoed around the kitchen. "So, if you know where I am, as well as who I am, are you in Johannesburg, too?"

"I was up until Christmas Eve. I, too, have been keeping myself busy. Ya know what they say about idle hands and all that. I have been doing jobs here and there for whoever wants to bankroll me for their particular cause at that particular time."

"Is that working out all right for ya?"

"Eh, it keeps me in pop tarts and Underoos. Nothing spectacular. I see that you are still doing the occasional job yourself. Last week I saw you walk into a therapist's office there in Johannesburg, and then three hours after you walked back out of there I'm hearing on the radio that – lo and behold – someone in said therapist's office suddenly dropped dead of a massive heart attack. You haven't missed a beat since Mexico City."

"Missed? No. However, when it comes to tidying up the loose ends from Mexico City, there is one beat that I did miss," Harper admitted.

"You referring to Chase?"

"I am referring to Chase. Why? Did I miss something else?"

"Not that I'm aware of, but if ya did, it won't segue into what I was calling you about nearly as nice."

"Oh," Rowe said in disappointment, "you didn't call just to catch up?"

"Afraid not. Sorry."

"You say with all the sincerity of Dick Cheney reloading his hunting rifle."

"So – about that," Devereaux went on, "you couldn't find Chase to tidy her up, but I did."

"What? You killed Laurie Chase?"

"I did not say that I killed her. I am just saying that she is one of the reasons that I was calling you. As it turns out, she is the secondary reason I called."

"If she's secondary then what is the primary reason you've reached out to me?"

Devereaux paused, took a deep breath, and then said, "Um, I kinda, sorta—"

"Spit it out, stammering studly."

"I need a favor."

Devereaux's Quandary

Harper Rowe thought he heard some movement coming from his bedroom. Moving the phone away from his ear, he took a long, intent listen. He heard nothing. Still, he waited a bit longer until he heard Kinley's voice rattle through the cell phone.

"Still there, Harp?"

Satisfied that the coast was clear and that Michelle was still soundly asleep, Harper put the phone back up to his ear. "Still here. You were saying?"

"Ya know how sometimes you pour too much milk on your Raisin Bran, and then the flakes get unenjoyably soggy, and you wish you could un-pour some of that milk?"

"Eerily so, yes. Where ya goin' with this, Kin?"

"Like I said, I need a favor. It's a pretty big favor."

"How big?"

"Let's just say that this favor is going to do for favors what King Kong did for gorillas."

"Ah geez," Harper said in exasperation, "how much milk did you pour this time, Dev?"

"This is something that I am relatively sure I couldn't ask of anyone else I know, or, for that matter, anyone else that has ever existed in the history of man."

"Spill it, milkman."

"I need you to get to JNB. You have a 5 a.m. flight to London. There's a tic–"

"Judas Priest, dude. That's less than an hour and a half from now."

"It's okay. You don't need to pack. In fact, it's probably best if you don't," Devereaux said matter-of-factly.

"You really know—"

"Like I was saying," Kinley continued, "there's a ticket waiting for you at the counter under the name of 'David Pleasance.' The 5 a.m. direct to London. Keep your head down from the security cameras in there. Once you land in London, you'll deplane, and there will be someone there waiting for you. They'll have one of those VIP signs with your name on it – well, not your name, but David Pleasance's name – and they will usher you to a private jet that will fly you at Mach 4 to Atlanta, Georgia."

"Atlanta? For real?" Harper asked. "Geez, Kin, I can't help but wonder if you can actually hear me furrowing my brow on my end of the phone here. What is this favor you're getting ready to ask of me, chief?"

"I need you to come to Atlanta and get arrested."

Harper was silent. He was not even breathing heavily.

"Harp?"

"Shh. I need you to be quiet while I scroll through my Rolodex of the drastically inane to be sure there isn't someone else you can ask to do this 'favor' you want done."

"Well, while you're doing that, I guess this is probably as good a time as any to add the addendum that I need you to not break any laws in the process."

"Okay. Just okay," Harper whispered harshly, now completely irritated. "I'm pretty sure this is the part where I totally turn off my thought process and just let you tell me exactly what's going on here,

Kinley. I swear on Oral Roberts' grave that if I didn't have to keep my voice down to keep my girlfriend from waking up and having me committed for still listening to your insanity, I'd be yelling the wax right out the other side of your ear."

"Remember the part of our conversation when I told you that I was doing jobs 'here and there'? And the part when I told you that I was in Johannesburg until a week ago?"

"Rings a bell, yes."

"I left Johannesburg to do a job just outside of Atlanta. Two nights ago I was doing just that: I was set up in the sixth floor of a downtown building, locked and loaded."

"So what went wrong?"

"I pulled the trigger and hit my target. Bang!!...assassin, baby. Done and done."

"And then someone started up the fan and took a crap?" Harper asked.

"Pretty much. I was getting ready to recoil my rifle, pack up, and hit the pavement, but I got spooked. Something made a ruckus behind me, and caused my normal steady self to lurch, which in turn sent my gun up against the side of the window, out of my hands, and down to the street below. What's even worse? When it landed, it fired again right into someone's car and set its stupid alarm off."

"Oh no."

"Yeah, that's pretty much what I said except that it started with a 'Sh' and ended with an 'it,' and then I ran like a man on fire down to street level."

"Hang on a second, Kin. I made myself some tea to help wake me up. It's boiling and I need both hands to deal with this. Can't put you on speaker phone because, well, it's almost 4 a.m. here. Naturally, I don't want to miss any of this riveting story, so just hang tight."

Harper set the phone down, grabbed the old-fashioned tea kettle before it began to whistle, put a teabag in a cup, poured water over it, picked up the phone, and sat down on one of the stools that Michelle had in her kitchen.

"Okay. I'm back."

"So I hit the sidewalk running, but I was too late. A crowd had already formed and the sirens of incoming cop cars told me it was time to wait and hide."

"Was your car close?"

"Yeah, so I sneaked away from the scene, got in my car, slid down in the seat and waited to see which cop from which precinct picked up my weapon and hauled it off."

"Well, it's nice to know that you're not above such second-grade tactics like slinking down in the seat of a car to hide from the cops."

"Well, dude. I saw what I needed to see."

"I'm sure ya did," Harper smiled as he took a sip from his cup of tea. "I'm also relatively sure that – reading in between the lines – I can see where my arrest comes into play – without breaking the law."

"You never let me down, kid."

"It's like that song says – I can get the punishment, but I just don't get to do the sin."

Devereaux let out a relieved chuckle. "I'll see you when that jet lands in about 17 hours."

"It'll be New Year's Eve. Don't think we'll have too much trouble getting me arrested."

SAYING GOODBYE

Harper walked back into the bedroom. He gently grabbed Michelle Runkle's shoulder and shook it.

"Hey, girlie."

"What?" she answered grumpily, without lifting her head from the pillow.

"I gotta go."

"Whatever," Michelle mumbled into her pillow.

"I mean, I'm going for good. I won't be back."

"Good, go," she said without rolling over.

"I'm going to make a water balloon and bust it over your head. You good with that? And then I'm going to steal all your silverware."

"Sounds good," Michelle said before drifting back to sleep.

And that was when Harper realized that he had been blessed with the one gift that all men pray for: an easy escape from a relationship.

He let go of Michelle's shoulder, went into the bathroom to brush his teeth, then collected the four things he had entered the relationship with – his wallet and the contents within, his passport, and two cell phones – and walked quietly out the front door.

He looked both ways before crossing the street, pulled up the collar on his shirt and headed off into the night.

ABOUT THE AUTHOR

Doc Ephraim Bates is the author of the popular
Boom!!...Killers. and Dragon's Men series.

He has been writing comedic action thrillers since age
fourteen. The youngest of seven sons, Doc mastered the
three skills most valuable to his characters: maintaining
a sense of humor, learning how to take a beating, and
the art of not getting caught.

Doc makes his online home at
www.docephraimbates.com

Connect with Doc on Facebook at
www.facebook.com/doc.bates.90

If the mood strikes you, send him an email at
doc@docephraimbates.com

Sign up for his occasional
and always-entertaining newsletter at
www.goldenalleypress.com/doc-ephraim-bates

www.ingramcontent.com/pod-product-compliance
Lightning Source LLC
Chambersburg PA
CBHW070447120726
47910CB00003B/959